# Seven Short Twists

To my muse,
who inspired me
to turn my quests, loves,
heartaches, dreams and imagination
into words, whether anyone
ever reads them
or not.

# Seven Short Twists

Short Stories

by Robert Simms

ISBN: 978-0-9834642-8-0
Published in the United States by
Robert F. Simms
Greer, South Carolina

# Contents

# The Hunt

Every rattle and shiver of the old Ford Bronco was music to Carl Hampton, because they meant that he had found the rare opportunity to leave the gladiatorial arena of big business, which he loved, and retreat to the woods to hunt deer, which he loved even more. In fact, even if Carl could have driven his Lincoln right up to the edge of the game reserve, he wouldn't have done it, preferring the rough, bumpy, noisy ride in the Bronco. After all, if you were going hunting, the experience had to be complete. And on a practical level, getting up at four o'clock in the morning so as to be in the forest at dawn, you needed the jolting ride of the Bronco to wake you up.

Hunting, he had thought frequently, was a metaphor for big business. You stalked game in both; you studied your game to know its habits, its weaknesses. You stayed ready, with the proper weapon and load, and disguised yourself so as not to appear dangerous. And in both, there came the moment to move in for the kill. That was so whether you were talking about selling toasters or looking for entire companies to buy. It was still a hunt.

Carl was nearly alone on the road at this hour, with only one other car having met him and one somewhere behind him since the last little town. Shortly, his lights illuminated the green and white sign that pointed off to the right and said simply, "Sec. 435," the game reserve's designation of one of sixteen hunting areas in this far northern reach of the state. Carl clutched and braked, and turned into the two ditches that passed for a road, his windshield instantly being slapped by tree branches that nearly obscured the trail. He hoped he would be the only hunter here in this section this morning. The car behind him may have carried hunters, but there were numerous roads into the large hunting acreage, and they might be miles away. He hoped so, because he planned not to wear the bothersome orange vest that distracted him, if not the deer.

About a hundred yards into the thick brush, he entered a small clearing, where he had parked his Bronco many times to begin his hunt. The weathered, nearly worn-out vehicle rocked side to side as it went over the lumpy surface, and then came to a halt at the end of the clearing. In the motionless air and the still inky gloom of the five o'clock hour, he got out, went around to the back of the four-wheel-drive rover, opened the hatch, and removed his 30.06 rifle. He slung it over his brown camouflage jacket, checked his ammunition supply, and then closed the hatch, and headed out into the brush, which quickly changed to moderately dense forest.

There wasn't any real hunting to be done for a little while, at least as long as it took to walk a quarter or half a mile. Still, he walked quietly, avoiding noisy leaves and carefully bending back branches and releasing them gradually as he went through underbrush.

He couldn't help chuckling over how equally stealthily he had come to the brink of what might be his ultimate business victory. A member of the board of Duncan Industries, he had been working for months to acquire the necessary stock to take over the company. He had finally reached 31%, with only one other block of stock to buy out to give him controlling shares. One man held 20% of the total stock, the next largest holding in the company. That man, who was now his "game" in the business hunt, was Lewis Parkland, a financier who made his fortune in construction and development, sold his sizeable company at the age of thirty-two, and helped start three banks in a row. Simultaneously, he began to run with the big dogs of the capital city, which included not only attending social events of the upper crust, but also adopting some of the more tempting personal pursuits of the rich and powerful.

It had been just those pursuits that had made Mr. Lewis Parkland such a vulnerable stockholder in Duncan Industries. As Carl Hampton had discovered about six months ago, Lewis had acquired not only one fifth of the stock of Duncan Industries, but also a petite blond mistress in the person of Alicia Duncan, daughter of Charles Duncan, founder of the company. She was twenty-seven, single, and managing the company's main office, while her older brother served as vice-president. Lewis Parkland was thirty-eight, muscular, bronzed, and rich. Daddy Duncan had no idea his daughter was in bed with his company's chief stockholder, nor did Lewis's wife. Carl Hampton knew, but only because he had hired the best P.I. in the state to dig up something, anything, on Parkland.

Exactly one week ago, the gumshoe had given his full report on Lewis Parkland. He was a hunter, like Carl, and spent just about every weekend stalking whatever was in season. But every other weekend of late, he packed his hunting gear, kissed his wife goodbye, set out to meet his hunting buddy John Poe for a weekend away, and then headed straight for Elder Mountain Lake, where he met Alicia Duncan. Included with the report, was graphic, if not artistic, photographic proof of Parkland's weekend hanky-panky, On those weekends, Lewis came home with sad tales of unsuccessful hunting. Oh, well, thought Carl, it depends on what the "game" was. Carl's game was Lewis Parkland; and now he knew his quarry's weakness.

Carl's plan was simple. Two days ago, Carl invited Lewis to meet him for lunch at the Tower Top, a revolving restaurant atop one of the city's several true skyscrapers. Parkland knew Hampton wanted to make yet another offer for his stock. Carl had treated him to several *very* expensive meals and outings, all designed to soften him up and talk him out of his shares. He planned, again, to refuse, with just a hint of reluctance, as if he really wanted to sell, but had other reasons keeping him from it. In actuality, he had no plans to sell to Mr. Carl Hampton, a fact that both he and Hampton knew. What he didn't know was what inducement Carl carried with him to lunch that day.

At lunch, Lewis was shown the contents of a manilla envelope, in full color. Carl said, in a very level tone and with a confident—and to any observant diners, friendly—smile, that in the event that Lewis decided to decline his latest offer for his stock, Carl was certain his wife and Mr. Duncan both would be interested in a small photographic exhibition. Lewis was able to maintain his cool, for the sake of the restaurant audience, though naturally he seethed and fumed underneath. He appeared to purse his lips in serious consideration of the offer, checked his calendar, and said with surprising control that he would meet with Carl Monday morning at his office, to make the transaction. Then, rising before his meal had arrived, he pleasantly called Carl Hampton an appropriately obscene name, and departed.

Carl finished his meal and half of Lewis's, and ordered French silk pie, and began anticipating the next board meeting, when he would assume the chair. It was sunrise on the fortunes of Carl Hampton. The profit hunt was just about to realize its most productive moment.

It was dawning in the reserve. Carl had come to the edge of a clearing, the site of prize kills in the past three years. Something about this clearing and the nearby glade drew deer like moths to porch lights, especially at sunup. The near edge of the clearing was bordered by a steep rise, with a rocky outcropping along the top, rimmed by the forest. From here, Carl could see the entire clearing, which was something like a gorge, containing perhaps a quarter of a square mile in total.

Six feet or so up on the top of a rock, with another two feet above him to crouch behind and steady his rifle on, Carl positioned himself slowly, grew still and relaxed, though ready, and waited for a ten-point buck to come out for a morning snack. An occasional twig breaking across from the clearing told him he wouldn't have to wait long. A similar sound behind him perhaps seventy-five yards told him he might have his choice of deer.

Ten minutes later, no more, a large buck nuzzled through the foliage directly across the clearing from his position. Carl only regretted his expedition would be brief. He would go home early. One clean shot would take the game. The graceful but skittish animal surveyed the sloping gorge from top to bottom, lifting his nose into the air several times to detect any sign of "man." Fortunately, the wind constantly rolled up through the clearing, carrying Carl's scent away.

After a moment, the deer cautiously stepped into the clearing, just the length of his body, his white tail still touching the brush behind him. Satisfied he could take breakfast in safety, he began to nibble near him. Carl waited for him to turn sideways, so he could aim for the heart. After about five minutes, finally he did. The range was about a hundred yards. Carl slowly and quietly turned a ring on his scope, then sighted the prize buck. He was in the cross hairs. Carl had been chambered and ready to fire since setting up nearly half an hour ago.

He steadied the rifle, lined up the cross hairs on the buck just behind the front quarters. His finger on the trigger, he began to put pressure on it, ever so slightly. And he thought about the primal realities. The buck was a survivor. So was man. And just as animals had their prey, man had his. All of life seemed to come down to moments like this, man against his prey, making the decision to take the kill when circumstance offered it. It was the way of life: life and death, hunter and prey, eat and be eaten, kill and be killed.

His finger tightened. The buck nibbled. The cross-hairs were fixed on his heart. The trigger gave way.

Carl didn't hear the shot, not at first. First, there was the impact, not a recoil to his shoulder, as usual, but in the middle of his back, and passing through his torso like lightning, bringing wind and red rain through the front of his jacket, stinging his hand and making away at the speed of sound from the rock in front of him. His rifle slid out from his disabled grip, over the boulder to the front, and fell fifteen feet to underbrush below. Everything went black, as his head fell forward to the rock, and Carl felt himself slump in place, sliding down the edge of the boulder, coming to rest on his back. He could not see it, but the buck had whipped around, shown his flag, and disappeared into the forest.

Carl ceased being aware of any feeling, though he believed he could hear the rustle of the trees, and the crunching of leaves. He drifted through various images in his mind, mostly just patches of light and dark, as he tried to climb up out of his confusion. No particular thought would come to mind, though he struggled to make sense of what had happened. He felt himself wafting away, getting lighter and lighter.

Somewhere out on a wave of unconsciousness, he heard their voices, as they gathered around him. If anyone touched him, he didn't know it. They just stood above him, in the dim gloom of the early morning.

"Congratulations, Lewis," said a feminine voice.

"Thank you, Alicia. It felt good," said the other. "But Carl here just had his weekend shot to hell."

And the voices, and the couple they belonged to, made diminishing sounds through the brush and woods, as they walked away.

But Carl Hampton melted into the mute consciousness of the life around him, and floated away on a tide going out, out, into the blackness of a new and unprecedented night. As he did, he heard his last thoughts replayed for review. He was going home early. Everybody was. One clean shot had taken the game.

# The Love Seat

Custom Staffing was an innovative and a profitable business, one that had multiplied since its founding fifteen years ago, and Richard Edwards, co-founder, frankly had made a killing at it. Now, doing business at the level of more than $18 million per year in three locations throughout the northeast, the company was expanding again, opening an office in Hart, a relatively small city on the perimeter of a metroplex three states away. Most of the groundwork had been done for the new location, and an associate in the Manhattan office was being transferred to head up the operation. But Richard, it had been decided, would be needed to help open the office, meet with their principal clients, and get the enterprise off to a rousing start.

That's why it happened that on this August afternoon Richard was boarding a plane to Hart, site of Hart College, his alma mater, and a place he had not visited since his graduation there sixteen years ago. He had received invitations to his ten-year reunion, but sent regrets to the planning committee. Business was too demanding, he had told himself, his wife, and others. And he was busy, no doubt about that, but not that busy. No, the reason lay in the bittersweet memories he had about Hart College.

He had chosen Hart because of its excellent accounting program. Richard's father headed a prominent Boston accounting firm, and Richard had long ago decided he would "do what his daddy did," and be an accountant. All this pleased daddy, of course, though he had never actually tried to lead Richard in that direction. But in response to his son's free decision, he had virtually offered him an opening salary of $65,000 per year, plus perquisites, adjusted, of course, for whatever inflation might do to the cost of living between the year Richard entered Hart College and the year he graduated.

So, off to Hart went Richard, leaving behind Susan Brooks, a nice but immature girlfriend still in high school, telling her he would write. He wrote for a year, but absence didn't make the heart grow fonder as it was supposed to, and he told her after that first year they each would be better off having someone nearby they could actually go out with.

Then, in the first month of his junior year, he met Meredith Anderson. She had been there his first two years, as well, but in the sea of feminine faces on the Hart campus she was just one more beautiful girl, and he hadn't noticed her except in the casual way that guys on campus do. But they were seated beside each other in a political science class that third year, and it was when she spoke that the casual was left behind.

Her voice was soft, and "fuzzy around the edges," as Richard told her later. And the first time she said, "Hi," Richard was smitten. They went Dutch on lunch in the campus grille that very noon, and from that moment, for the rest of their college careers, they were inseparable. And it was no ordinary love story.

Perhaps other couples at Hart College and elsewhere were as much in love and as passionate about each other and as deeply philosophical and intensely poetic and as giddily happy and as lost in each other as were Richard and Meredith, but he couldn't imagine they were. This was unique. It was a classic among classics. It was beyond reality.

It was ideal.

They did the commonplace and the unusual with each other. They met for five-minute snacks between classes, and spent long hours walking through the acres of woodland belonging to the college. They went to crowded, noisy fraternity parties, and sat alone by Lohmann Pond nearby, just looking into each other's eyes.

Richard had never met anyone like Meredith. She had thrown herself into their relationship with phenomenal, selfless abandon. She would do anything for Richard.

She bought him things. In fact, he was sometimes embarrassed at her generosity; but until he started pulling down sixty-five grand a year, he really wasn't well off, having preferred to make do on his 10-hour per week campus job for spending money, since his dad was already footing the bill for tuition and other costs. But if Meredith ever felt awkward about spending money on him, she never showed it. She bought him sweaters and shoes, books and funny little souvenirs, cologne and gas for his car.

There was nothing she wouldn't do for Richard, within the bounds of propriety, of course, and Richard was astoundingly proper and virtuous toward her. They had their late-night trysts, like most students, and they spent their share of evenings in secluded places here or there holding each other and yearning for more intimacy than either of them felt was moral and proper to have. But somehow, through those two years of intensely passionate togetherness, honored even by the campus newspaper as the romance voted most likely to become immortal, they followed the values of their upbringing and faith, and never really regretted it. After all, they fully expected to consummate their love in marriage.

The ticket line at the boarding gate was moving, and

Richard moved up with it, all of three feet. He peered out the window at the nose of the jet aircraft, being fueled for the two-hour flight, and thought about that song "Leavin' on a Jet Plane," and how it had always made him feel. It was the way he had felt years before, about Meredith.

For they had really expected to get married. But it never happened. For while Meredith would do virtually anything for Richard, there was one thing she would not change her mind about. As a little girl, she had had a sister who required "special education," and since she was nine or so Meredith, always tenderhearted, had dreamed of being a special education teacher someday. She came to Hart to study education and specialize in what was now called learning disabilities. And if there was anything she poured herself into with passion other than her deep love of Richard, it was her career goal.

In itself, this didn't affect their future at all, but what she had always seen herself doing was returning home to Collinburg, a small town barely twenty-five miles away, and teaching the many disabled students where she had grown up. Besides, she hated big cities. And that was where the rift began.

Richard was resolute about becoming an accountant, and especially about joining his father's firm with the security it brought with it. As his college years wore on, he was even more certain that he wanted to spend not one more day in poverty; and sixty-five thousand a year was a nice place to start being comfortable. Richard's older brother Chip had gone to Boston College and then attempted to start a retail business, and had failed miserably. By the time Richard went to Hart, Chip was selling clothes at a local Boston mall, barely making ends meet. Richard was certain he had no more entrepreneurial ability than Chip, though he had certainly had the mind for the figures.

Richard and Meredith had discussed future plans from the first, and both had gradually revealed their abiding commitments to their respective dreams. But somewhere in both their minds, because they loved each other so much, they both believed the other would one day, out of the blue, give up his or her dream, or modify it drastically, in a sacrificial gesture for their joint happiness. Instead, they began having more and more short discussions in which their mutual intractableness became apparent. Neither was "stubborn," of course, and they had the sense, and the understanding of each other to concede that they were possessed of powerful and deeply rooted dreams. Nevertheless, they discussed (they never "argued") the rationale behind their commitments, and each tried to make the other see the wisdom of changing his mind.

As April of their senior year arrived, however, neither had really reconsidered, and they found themselves looking at graduation three weeks away, and facing, for the first time in two years, the probability that they would get their diplomas, pack their bags, travel in opposite directions a thousand miles apart, and never see each other again. And though it was making them both miserable, there didn't seem to be any solution.

By the middle of their last semester, Richard had not made any moves toward investigating a prospective business site in Collinburg, or even toward hunting a position with an existing firm. And Meredith had not contacted any schools in Boston, though Richard had gone to the trouble to provide her with a list he had researched in January. Instead, Meredith had had several interviews with principals and schoolmasters in Collinburg and the surrounding county, and had been virtually assured that upon graduation she would have a modestly paid position fulfilling her heart's dream. Richard, for his part, had been taking care of preliminaries with his dad, and had given him every indication that he intended to join the firm in June. To the questions his father and mother had asked him frequently about what he and Meredith were planning, Richard simply said that it wasn't "settled" yet. There was still time, technically. And during the last week of April, they talked about it, cried about it, worried about it, every day.

Meredith insisted that Richard would have plenty of business in Collinburg, and she was certain he would be successful from the start. Richard's heart ached as he told her he was equally certain he didn't have what it took to start a new business, and besides, his father would be broken-hearted. She, on the other hand, he proposed, would have her pick of schools in Boston, where there were surely many more special students than in Collinburg. Meredith countered that she belonged in Collinburg; and she admitted her painful ambivalence, because she also felt in her heart that she belonged with Richard. Richard said he felt the same way, but that he felt his life, and their lives, were in Boston. And that's where the discussion stayed.

That's why on May 1, two weeks before final exams and three before graduation, Richard and Meredith were at an impasse, and why, that afternoon, they were sitting silently on the south lawn of the administration building of Hart College, looking down at their hands. They were in a little cast-iron love seat, like other lawn furniture scattered here and there around the campus. It was the only one of its kind, though, and sat underneath an oak tree that graced the lawn. Sitting there, as they had dozens of times holding hands and breathing in synchrony, they had looked out on the campus, their wonderland setting, and had dreamed of their lives together. Today, they sat in mute depression, facing emptiness.

"Can I help you?" said the ticket agent, and Richard was jerked briefly out of reverie and fumbled for his ticket, handing it to the uniformed woman. She marked and stamped and tore at it, and handed it back reshuffled and stuffed, wishing him a nice flight. Boarding having begun, he headed for the gate, and walked down the corridor that led to the hatch of the aircraft. He mumbled a hello to the flight attendant checking boarding passes, and moved to first class, taking his window seat and immediately gazing out the port at nothing in particular, continuing to play back for his mind the events of that day sixteen years ago.

The night before that May 1, Richard had sat in his dorm room being very practical—someone had to be—and very emotionally controlled, thinking through a decision that would have to be made. He considered briefly, very briefly indeed, the option of just graduating, pledging to write, visiting Meredith as often as he could, and hoping something would change. But his long distance romance with Susan three years before had not worked, and he was afraid that if he attempted it with Meredith, they would simply grow apart, find other people, and go through a long, drawn-out love-death like dying of cancer. That, he was certain, would be far more painful than a short, quick stroke. And he was just as certain that, even if Meredith had reasoned out the same thing, she would not be able to give the word. Somebody had to. It fell to Richard to say goodbye.

The plane lifted off the ground, its landing gear bumping underneath as it retracted. Richard watched the houses underneath him grow smaller and smaller, the highways populated with toy cars, the little lakes beginning to look like gleaming puddles on the lawn of the receding land. How like what time did to the past, except that for Richard, spending this time in vivid recall of that day sixteen years ago, the details were magnified, as if they had happened only yesterday.

That May 1, he had met her after a class—they shared none that semester—and suggested they go sit under the oak tree, if nobody else had beaten them to the love seat. No one had, and they skipped their next class by mutual, though unexpressed consent. Small talk took up the first ten minutes, but both of them knew that time and the future were pressing hard on them.

Richard made it short. "Meredith, I always thought we would wind up going the same way together. I can't believe we're not. I don't want to go home to Boston just to write you letters for a year and then have us grow apart. I'm ready to start a life, right now. I want you to start it with me. Will you? Will you go with me to Boston?"

"Richard," she said in that fuzzy, and now distressed and grief-filled tone, "I can't. Go with me," she urged softly and quietly.

"I can't." Richard gazed into her eyes, saw her sadness, her desire, her awareness of impending hurt. His voice lower, softer too, and breaking beneath its control, he told her, "Then let's say goodbye. I don't want to. But what else can we do." It was not a question.

Meredith looked at him, motionless, having known this moment was coming. Little pools gathered in her eyes, and one of them spilled over and ran down her cheek, dripping to her blouse. Almost imperceptibly, she nodded her assent, and in a whisper almost without voice, she said, "I will always love you, Richard." Then she got up, and walked away, across the grass, toward her dormitory, at a steady but normal pace. After she had gone twenty yards, Richard had the impulse to run after her, embrace her, tell her to forget he had said anything, that he would go with her, go with her anywhere, do anything, be poor, be a failure, just as long as they could be together. But he didn't move, knowing that the notion was foolish. After fifty yards or so, Meredith broke into a run, her right hand flying to clasp her mouth, to hold in the tearful cries Richard could already hear bursting out, echoing from the brick walls of the campus buildings, and ringing in his ears. Then, the pains in his breast throbbed unmercifully, and he broke down in great heaves of grief, sobbing into his hands, little streams of tears descending to the lattice of the little love seat, and onto the grass below.

Richard didn't see Meredith the next two weeks. She appeared in none of the places they had customarily met each other. Apparently she didn't eat in the dining hall or the grille, because he often stayed more than an hour to catch a glimpse of her, perhaps to see if she were holding up, or maybe even to tempt himself with the idea of undoing what he had done, even then. But she never showed.

The last day of exams, he asked a friend of hers if she had seen Meredith, and learned that she had left for Collinburg that day, having made arrangements to have her diploma mailed to her. She was beginning her teaching job in the summer session, and had gone home early to rent an apartment so she could establish a place on her own, and to get ready to begin work in June.

She was really gone. And he knew he'd never see her again. Richard took his diploma with calm dignity, ate a celebration dinner with his parents, who had flown out for the event, and only then told them he and Meredith had gone their separate ways. They commiserated with him, but couldn't have known what he was going through. They, like all parents, had never been young and in love.

They tried to cheer him, making light conversation, catching him up on the news from home, so he would be up to speed when he got back, which would be in two days. And, they mentioned that Susan Brooks had stopped by, just to say "hi," a week or so ago, and that she had mentioned in passing that she was working at Bradshaw Insurance Company as a secretary, and that she hadn't found anybody to take Richard's place in her life yet. Richard found it odd that Susan would have just "dropped by" his parents' house, and even more suspicious that she would have just "happened" to mention that she still wasn't married.

The day after graduation, Richard saw his parents off at the Hart County airport, as they returned to Boston. Then he went back to campus, and packed all his belongings into a U-Haul trailer. Before leaving, he took a last look at the Hart College campus. He walked to the south lawn, and looked out toward the great oak tree, in the middle of the now nearly deserted campus grounds. The little, white wrought-iron love seat sat under the shade, unoccupied, except for the lingering image of two lovers who spent two years in a dream world never imagining they would sit there and finally say goodbye.

Then Richard turned, sighed resolutely, walked back to his car, and drove the two-day trip home, to his career and his life. And it just so happened that when he got there, Susan Brooks just happened to drop by again, just in time to help him unpack, and to merit an invitation to supper as a reward. Then she sat around all evening, as they all did, and talked about everything that had been happening in Boston.

By the middle of the next week, Richard had an apartment two miles away, and a date, quite to his own surprise, with Susan. He found that the spark was still there, and within a month it had been fanned into full flame. By

September, they were married.

"Ladies and gentlemen," said the captain's voice, "we're about to begin our descent into the Hart County Airport. Local conditions are cloudy and about 65°. We'll be passing through a cloud bank in a moment, and then landing on schedule at 3:20 local time. Thanks for flying with us, and we hope you return soon."

Richard looked out as the craft began plunging into the airborne cotton balls, and thought of how his life had been in the clouds since that first year with his father's firm. In fact, he had brought in so much new business, saved (and made) his clients so much money, and earned so many bonuses, that by the end of May nearly a year later he was the equivalent of rookie of the year. In addition, Susan turned out to be just the healing balm and inspiration he needed, and seemed to bring out in him the drive he had always lacked to really succeed.

It was during that first year that he met Jerry Barnhouse, who lived in the same apartment complex, and ran his own computer consulting and software development firm. Barnhouse was to computer programs what Richard was to accounting, and together they dreamed up the perfect combination of their skills to make money: Custom Staffing, a staff leasing company. Ironically, Richard Edwards, who had always believed himself to have little or no entrepreneurial ability, left his father's firm, moved to New York, and started a business one year after graduating from Hart College. His parents were disappointed that he would be moving, but he and Jerry had determined that New York was the best place to begin, and the decision proved to be phenomenally correct. In its fourth year of operation, Custom Staffing grossed more than $8 million, and by its tenth year, had opened two more offices in the northeast.

Now, they were expanding again, opening an office in Hart. Strangely enough, Richard had not come up with the idea, exactly. He and Jerry had hired an outside consulting firm to study the matter of their expansion and recommend a location in the central or southeast part of the U.S. The study came up with Hart, which served a major metroplex having the greatest market for their service.

As the silver airliner broke through the cloud cover, it was little more than a thousand feet off the ground, and Richard could look out toward the west from the airport and see the city, sprawling over miles of gently rolling hills. He saw the lofty spire of the Hart College tower, and the roofs of surrounding college buildings. Soon, they melted into the compressing skyline as the jet airplane descended toward the runway.

From the airport, Richard rented a car and drove straight to his hotel. Reviewing his schedule, he told himself he wouldn't have time to go over and visit the college. He had to have dinner with the new office staff that evening, open the business tomorrow, meet with the three major client firms already on board that afternoon, dine with the manager alone tomorrow evening, and then return to New York the following day, Wednesday. The only thing was, his flight on Wednesday wasn't until three o'clock. That gave him all morning and noon to spend in Hart, and nothing to do. Nothing, that is, except visit the college.

With two hours before his supper meeting with the staff (there in his hotel for convenience), he lay back on the hotel room bed and continued to muse about his past, and the girl who had made it so bittersweet. Nothing was wrong with his nearly sixteen-year marriage. He loved Susan warmly and devotedly, and she him. It was just that the chapter with Meredith had not closed satisfactorily, and she had never really left his mind. He thought about the little white love seat, and wondered if it were still there. It had probably rusted and been replaced, he thought. Still, it would be interesting to see. He realized it would also bring up many feelings he probably didn't want to experience all over again, but something was beginning to grip him and drive him to go see it. Maybe he needed to relive the memory in order to be done with it. Of course, feeding his nostalgia might also be a guarantee that it would haunt him for years to come. But it was a risk he decided to take.

The business of his trip was concluded with astonishing rapidity. The next day flew by, with glad-handing and ceremony and hoopla. He ate too much at all the meals, and stayed up too late watching cable movies Tuesday night. But Wednesday morning arrived, and he checked out of the hotel and drove over to Hart College about ten o'clock.

The first thing that impressed him was how little had changed. The college had the character of ivy league schools that cherish tradition, and so had maintained its classic look through the years. There was one new building, but off to one side of the familiar grouping of original edifices.

Richard parked his rental and walked down the central sidewalk between the major buildings. At the end, he went down the granite steps beside the administration building, and around to the back, where he could see the dormitories, on the far side of the south lawn. There, in the middle of the football-field-sized lawn, was the large and now larger oak tree, casting its huge shadow. Underneath, in the cool, dark circle, was the love seat.

Richard stood there for a moment, just peering at it, seeing himself and Meredith Anderson sixteen and seventeen years ago, just as they were then, lost in love. He turned and walked into the building, pretending he didn't really want to go out to the tree. Down the long hall running the length of the building he passed the cafeteria and the grille, now deserted after the summer sessions, and looked in to see the familiar booths where he had eaten so often with Meredith.

At the other end of the hall, he exited the building on the far side, and took a right, going around to the back of the building again, where he could see the south lawn from another angle. There was the tree, its branches hanging low. The love seat was behind one of them, deep in the shade of the tree, and deep in the recesses of his mind and heart.

It was as much a psychological and spiritual yearning that drew him to the seat as it was the weak reasoning that it would be therapeutic. He went down the matching granite steps on this side of the building and made his way down the sidewalk toward the great tree. On the way, he panned his eyes and took in the library, Talbert Hall, and the business building. All was the same, as if it had been yesterday. Within twenty-five yards or so of the tree, he had moved enough to the side of the low-hanging branch to see the love seat again, and he had begun to head toward it, across the grass, when he realized that while he had been in the administration building, someone had sat down in the seat.

He stopped, and was about to think of what he might do for a few minutes to kill time while waiting for the love seat to become vacant again, when a shiver and a heart-stopping moment of recognition came over him. Unless he were dreaming, or making up things out of the longing of his heart, the figure in the love seat was Meredith.

As soon as she and the love seat had become visible to him, he had become visible to her, and she looked up from her reverie and removed all doubt that it was she. There was a subtle look of shock on her face, if such a thing can be subtle. For she was clearly surprised, but in a way that suggested that deep inside she had expected something like this to happen.

Richard, however, had not. He was certain his own shock was extremely conspicuous. He could feel the blood run out of his face, and his head began to swim. It seemed like ten minutes before he regained the presence of mind to speak, but by then he didn't want to, just yet.

Instead, he walked very slowly over to the love seat. Ten feet away, he paused, peering into those eyes now locked on him, those eyes that had so often probed his soul when they told their love and shared their dreams so eloquently and silently when time stood still for them both. All he could manage was, "Hello Meredith."

"Richard. Hi," she said, in her fuzzy tone that had not changed substantially. "I dreamed you would be here."

Richard had not been prepared to see her after all these years, and certainly had not expected her to say anything like that.

"What do you mean, dreamed?" he asked.

"I dreamed it, at night, two days ago," she said, unblinking and wide-eyed, a sure sign of her sincerity. Richard stood there contemplating that pronouncement, and finally decided to change the subject.

"I came out on business."

"What kind of business?"

"My own. Staff leasing. I... I went into business for myself, with a partner, several years ago." He didn't tell her it was fifteen years ago, remembering how firmly he had vowed he could never make it in business for himself.

"What in the world brought you here, at this moment, of all moments in time," said Richard, almost under his breath.

"I told you. I dreamed it. I was here and you were here. I came. It's the first time I've been back since that day." She didn't need to identify the day more precisely than that.

"You look good," he said, "so good." It was an inane thing to say, but it was certainly true, and he was trying to say how much he had thought about her, and yearned for her. Apparently, it communicated, because she responded in kind.

"I've thought of you every day," she said, shaking her head side to side with finality.

It made him feel guilty, but no more than he had felt for years, ever since he made the decision to say goodbye.

"Can I sit down?" he said.

"Silly! Of course you can. Why else are you here?" She slid over and he sat down gently beside her. It felt right, though terribly awkward at the same time. He kept his hands on his knees, looked at them for a moment, and then looked up at her.

"I guess I should catch up on you," he stated with quiet cheerfulness. "What are you doing, now?"

"Still teaching," she said smiling, as if he should have known the answer.

"Married?" he asked, trying to sound casual, knowing he wasn't convincing.

"Yes. He's a lot like you." Her voice was soft, whispery, girlish. "But he's not you."

Richard shut his eyes, feeling both continued guilt and a wash of appreciation and affection, at this obvious expression of her deathless love.

"What about you," she said, "married, I guess?"

"Yeah," said Richard, almost embarrassed, then with a slight chuckle, "hometown girl."

"Boston babe, huh?" she returned, with light humor.

"Yeah," he said, in the same attitude, and then more seriously, "and not much like you at all, actually."

"You'll never meet anybody like me, Richard, as long as

you live."

"I know that all too well. And I knew it then, Meredith. I hope you know that." Richard fiddled with his fingers a moment, and then started to add a thought: "I wish . . . "

"Don't," she said. "Don't wish. There'll never be anybody who can take your place for me. But I don't make myself miserable wishing. Still, not a day goes by that I don't think of you."

Feeling too powerfully caught up in the moment to continue the course of conversation they were following, Richard retreated to the less intimate. "Well, I told you what I was doing here. Now, what brings you here?"

"I flew, actually," she said slyly, and then added, "And I told you, I came because I dreamed about our meeting here."

"You flew? From Collinburg? Twenty-five miles?"

"No, silly. Oh, I didn't tell you." Her face flushed even more with embarrassment. "I didn't stay in Collinburg. I taught there for a year, then I met some people at a conference I went to; that led to an offer at a bigger school with a lot better pay, and I moved away."

Richard almost glared at her, more in incredulity than hostility. "You told me, you avowed to me, that you *belonged* in Collinburg. And you moved away?" He felt the faintest sense of frustration come too late, as he realized that she, too, had turned around after school and done what she tearfully told him she couldn't do—leave her hometown. "I was sitting here feeling bad because *I* went home, worked a year, and then did what I told you I couldn't do—start a business! You moved away?" he repeated in amazement.

"I know," she confessed, not looking at him for the moment, instead studying her own feet, as he had done earlier in shame. "I didn't plan it that way. I couldn't have known it would happen that way. So, you don't have to feel bad. At least, not alone."

It took a few moments to deal with this sudden revelation. Nothing was really changed, as far as he could see, except his impression of the past. He had envisioned her all these years living the small-town life in Collinburg, helping the few students who came through the public schools she and her parents before her had attended. All along, she had been somewhere else.

They sat quietly for a minute or more. Richard realized it was pointless to serve up any more guilt over their mutual failure to carry through with their stubbornness. Instead, he mused about a crazy fantasy he had fought off frequently since college, when he became heartsick for his past and for her.

"Did you ever wonder," he said, "what you would do... I mean, I love my wife, and I don't wish anything would happen to her; but did you ever have the crazy thought *what if?* What if something happened to your husband, and something happened to my wife? God forbid, of course, and I'm not—you know. But what if it did? Would we look each other up?" And he added, in dead earnest, "I know I would. Would you?"

Meredith, a glowing, romantic smile stretching across her flushed cheeks, said, "In a New York minute."

Richard laughed. "Me, too!" and he wondered where she picked up the lingo of the Big Apple.

"For sixteen years, I've wondered what really would have happened, if we— " and then he realized he had to take the fall for this alone— "If *I* had at least told you I'd try writing, or coming to see you when I could. Maybe, since I wound up starting a business and you wound up moving away from Collinburg, we might have realized we could both have our separate dreams, and our dream of being together, too."

Richard gazed at her azure eyes, and added, "I guess I didn't really come here so much for business as I did because even though I was the one who said goodbye, I don't think I ever really let you go." For the first time, Richard's eyes were beginning to glaze over with moisture.

"And to answer your question, finally," she said to him in a low, calm voice, "that's why I came. I told you I dreamed you'd be here. So I came, so you could let go of me."

He could see she was being completely serious, and though he didn't have a clue as to how she could have had a dream about his being here, he understood what she was trying to say. But she explained her comment herself.

"I don't blame you for what happened. I *did,* at first, but not anymore. And I don't want you to blame yourself, either. I loved you, as no one did. I still love you, for who you were, and who you are in my memories. But I knew that wherever you were all these years, down deep you were probably eating yourself up, worrying about what could have been. And if you were married, I knew you weren't as free as you needed to be to love your wife the way you loved me. And I *do* want you to love her the way you loved me, I do, Richard. We went our separate ways, and nothing can bring the past back to us; and what we had is a part of that past. We would ruin it, or ruin other people's lives, if we tried to get it back. That's why we have to let *each other* go. We will always love each other, in that special place in our hearts that belongs only to us. But live your life, Richard. And love your wife, all the more, because of what we had. Will you do that for me?"

Richard had sat rapt, soaking in her quiet wisdom, wondering what gave her such mature discernment. He sensed that she had acquired some revelation of sorts, for just this moment, perhaps as a part of the dream she spoke of, but that however much she wanted him to love another, it wasn't for any lack of love for him herself. Realizing that, he suddenly felt at peace, about that day in the love seat long ago, about sixteen years of unfulfilled longings, about life in the present with his wife, whom he *did* love, so help him. Looking at Meredith, a wave of relief passed over his face, softened and smoothed out his expression, and spoke to her of his acceptance of her eloquently stated truth. Something in her own look said they could leave each other, now, and not look back with regret.

"I promise," he nodded, "with all my heart." After holding the moment for a long pause, he looked at his watch. "I have to catch a plane. I think I really know why I was here, now. Thank you, Meredith."

"Thank *you*, Richard, for some of the happiest hours of my life," she said, and then lifted her hand, and wriggled her fingers in the cute goodbye wave she had often given him at her dormitory door.

Richard whispered goodbye, and strode away, not looking back, feeling light and serene.

The flight back to New York that Wednesday afternoon was uneventful, and on time, thankfully. As she usually did when Richard flew, Susan Brooks Edwards, the hometown girl and "Boston babe," met him at the airport, kissed him hello and took his arm as they picked up his one bag, navigated the terminal, and drove home. Embracing her that night, he felt the richness of every love he ever experienced, bundled like a gift for this one who had shared his youth and waited for him to come home a man.

It was not to anyone else, in any way, that he gave his love to her; she was no surrogate for loves gone by. He was free to belong to her, more than he ever had been, though she had perhaps never been aware why he often seemed distant and melancholy. As he lay in the dark, late into the night, basking in the moonlight coming in ribbons through the blinds of their bedroom, he felt the weight of the past dissolve into peace, and saw the portal of his future swing wide with release.

It was in the newly found strength of this resolved grief of his youth that Richard was able to deal maturely with the notice that caught his eye in the metro section of the newspaper Thursday morning. There, on a page he ordinarily skipped, at his age, his eyes caught on a small paragraph, that he would save, and that would ever after haunt him:

> **Meredith A. Gray,** *Queens*
>
> Meredith Caroline Anderson Gray, 38, of 187 Lanford Lane, died Tuesday, August 10, after a brief illness.
>
> Mrs. Gray is the former Meredith Anderson of Collinburg, and a graduate of Hart College. She taught learning disabled students in Queens schools for fifteen years.
>
> Memorial services are Thursday, in Collinburg, at the Parkwood Presbyterian Church.

Richard never told anyone what had happened, or whom he had seen, that August 11 afternoon in Hart, or with whom he sat in the little white love seat under the oak tree, who had in fact died the day before. No one would have believed him, anyway.

# The Offer

It had been a lovely August evening of mingling, dining, conversation, and cultured revelry, all in the Tudor surroundings of Harold Wickenham's palatial home in the Kingston Hills Estates. Harold and his lovely wife Karen had hosted their seventh annual gathering for the firm of Wickenham, Barton and Sykes, and all the partners and junior partners and their spouses had dutifully attended. Not that any would have missed the occasion, for Wickenham always put on the dog, and no one ever went home sorry. The food beat any restaurant in the three-state area, and there was entertainment to boot, this year in the form of a madrigal group which also performed sketches from various works of Shakespeare.

David Trent had come alone, there being no Mrs. David Trent, and dates not being welcome at such a formal occasion. It was David's first event at the Wickenham's, his having been taken on as a junior partner only the previous May. He was the only unattached person at the party, except for John "Skitch" Parkins, whose wife had died tragically two years ago.

And now the proceedings were winding down, and the clock in the front hall was striking 11:30 as the madrigals could be heard loading their equipment into their van under the cover of the side driveway entrance, and Mr. Barton Esq. and wife were making their exit speeches at the front door, as Harold and Karen saw them out. David caught a glimpse of them engaging in their gracious and practiced pleasantries, Mrs. Barton fawning over Karen Wickenham, the arrangements, the decorations, the service, the food, the lawn, and anything else she could think of, as Marvin Barton simply smiled at Harold, and affirmed that he would indeed be "in" the next morning. David watched as Karen Wickenham, who was Mr. Wickenham's second and much younger wife, fairly beamed at Mrs. Barton, displaying a grace and natural beauty that seemed to exude from her pores, which, he had noticed during the evening, were themselves flawless.

There were only two junior partners and Mr. Sykes left, and all were preparing to get up from their seats in the library, where they had been enjoying suspiciously Cuban-like cigars offered to them earlier in an unlabelled box and having no ring bands to identify them. David began moving toward the door as well, having lingered only to continue to admire the beauty of the Wickenham home and of Mrs. Wickenham, who was probably no older than his own thirty-two years, though Harold was fifty-eight.

At the door, he attempted a parting greeting of warm and courteous neutrality toward Karen Wickenham, considerably less warm, however, than the conversation he always attempted to strike up with her when she visited the firm on occasion. She returned his compliments about the evening with an equally warm and courteous tone, lacking the interest in him that he allowed himself to believe she had expressed in their previous meetings at the law office, or at the Barton's home, where the month before they had conversed around the pool during a less formal, firm barbecue. But as he took her hand in a parting gesture, he believed he felt her give him some sort of signal.

And of course, he would shake Mr. Wickenham's hand, before thanking him for a wonderful evening, and expressing delight at the privilege of working with such a wonderful family of friends, etc, etc. Mr. Wickenham had just turned to him, after wishing Mr. Barton a good night. Instead of taking his hand, Wickenham put his hand on David's shoulder.

"David, it was great to have you here, tonight. You've been a real asset to the firm, too, I want you to know that."

"Thank you, sir," David managed with ease, "There's no better firm in the state to be working for."

"You are both correct and politically sagacious," Harold said, chuckling at the junior partner's flattery. "David, I have something I want to give you before you go. Do you have a minute?"

David donned a curious expression, looked quizzically at Karen, back at Harold, nodded agreeably, and said, "Of course."

"Good. Come up to my second-floor study. Karen, excuse us for a moment." He led the way up the three-landing staircase, across a deep oriental carpet, and into a "study" which was more like another library, illuminated around the cornices with recessed warm-tint fluorescent lighting. Harold, Mr. Wickenham to David, motioned to one of two comfortable side chairs in front of the four by eight foot desk at the window, and he himself went to the reclining desk chair behind it. Sitting down, he picked up a half-packed pipe, opened a humidor, finished the pack, selected a gold lighter, and turned the brimming tobacco into a lacework of fire. He enjoyed the first two puffs deeply, sent their remaining aromatic billows toward the ceiling, looked up thoughtfully into the cloud, reclined slightly, and then swivelled toward David. David watched the ritual, recognizing it as the accompaniment of some sort of conversation of importance. Wickenham had several pipes at the office as well, and used them in a similar manner when imparting significant truths and wise observations to junior partners and paralegals.

"Did you enjoy yourself tonight, David?" he asked with genuine interest.

"Absolutely. Wonderful time," David said with his smoothest delivery.

"I'm glad. I know there are people in my position, bosses, employers, who give parties only because they are expected to, but I honestly enjoy seeing our partners come to know each other, and have a time to be friends, not just lawyers and co-workers. I feel that way about you, David, just as much as anyone who's been with the firm twenty-five years."

"Thank you, Mr. Wickenham. I've never doubted the sincere friendship you have expressed toward me. It's one of the reasons I like the firm so much."

"Aside from how rich we're making you, eh?" said Wickenham, his grin betraying the dry humor that characterized him.

"Of course," said David, knowing that Mr. Wickenham was all too happy to have increasingly wealthy and consequently happy partners in his firm.

"Happy. Satisfied. That's something we all want. I'm glad to be an important part of that in the lives of the people of our firm." Wickenham settled his pipe in its holder, rose, gazed out the window briefly, then turned casually toward David. "I asked you up here not to give you anything, really, David, but to offer you something."

David wouldn't even have considered the possibility that he would be offered the position of full partner so early in his career, and the thought did no more than sail over his head as he wondered what Harold might be talking about.

"I have noticed on other occasions, and tonight, that you find Karen, my wife, to be a pleasant and attractive woman," Harold Wickenham said. And as he said it, David shuddered to his core, realizing that his interest in Karen Wickenham had been too obvious, so obvious as to attract his boss's attention, so obvious that now he was sitting on the opposite side of his boss's desk, waiting for the boom to be lowered, just seconds after thinking to himself that he was on an upward and glorious path to success. All of it shattered in a moment of disclosure.

That flash of heat and nervousness that seared him inwardly and sent shivers through his ribs and down into his pelvis made him feel weak and in need of the bathroom. He realized he was not blinking, and was staring rather blankly at Harold Wickenham, waiting for the other shoe to drop, for the quiet but efficient words of execution to emanate from the chief lawyer's mouth.

Instead, Harold Wickenham continued in the same tone of voice, so far lacking any sort of hint of remonstrance or censure.

"I note, as well, that she finds you interesting, and, I'm sure, attractive," said Harold. And then, noticing that David's face had visibly blanched, he interjected, "Oh, don't let it disturb you that I noticed, David. Really, there isn't much going on in the firm anywhere that I don't know about, and I would have known, as well, if there were anything more to it than circumstantial and mostly visual interest. If there had been, perhaps my attitude would have been different, tonight, but then again, perhaps not so different after all."

"Sir, I assure you, I—" David began. But Harold put up his hand gently, and with a reassuring look, cut him short.

"That's all right, David, you don't need to answer just yet. Let me finish, first." Harold paused, gathered his thoughts during another glance out the window, and then continued, almost haltingly, as if nervous about what he was about to 'offer,' as he said.

"I'm really rather glad Karen finds you interesting, and that you find her, uh, the same. It suggests to me that there may be a solution to something that has troubled me greatly over the past several years."

David was now thoroughly confused. Wasn't Mr. Wickenham saying he knew David lusted for his wife, and that he knew that she lusted (David believed) for him? Why wasn't he angry? What kind of game was he playing?

"You know, David, that I am nearly sixty. My wife is only thirty-three." Hmm, only a year older, David thought, and then slapped himself on his mental wrist for pursuing his lust during a conversation, or rather, a monologue, about it.

"I love Karen very much," Harold continued. "I want her to be happy. But there are some things I can't do for her, things that would make her happy. Things that a husband ought to do," he said, almost blurting the words out with embarrassment, as he turned to the window and looked out with what appeared to be extreme self-consciousness. "And it grieves me greatly that I cannot make her happy in that way."

David was stunned. It was evident that Mr. Wickenham was talking about sex, and equally evident that he was saying—could he really be saying?—that he was impotent. David found it incredible, shocking, that Wickenham was actually confessing such a thing about himself, much less to be doing so to a junior partner whom he didn't know well, and one whom he had suspected of having his sights on his wife. He didn't know what to think.

"Am I communicating," said Harold Wickenham, "I know I'm being a bit vague."

"No, I mean yes," said David, "I think I understand what you're saying. But sir, I am somewhat uncomfortable about talking about it. I mean, not about *it,* but about *you* and *it.* If you know what I mean."

Harold chuckled, relieving their joint tension slightly. "We're both talking around the thing, aren't we!" He sat down, puffed on his pipe once, returned it to the holder, knitted his fingers on the desk, twiddling them slightly, and continued.

"Let me be direct, David. How would you like to take my wife to bed?" He stopped twiddling, looked David in the eye, and dead panned.

"What?" David almost whispered, and then disguised a gulp. "I mean, sir, I don't know what you mean. Well, I know what you mean, but I hope you didn't think that I would ever have tried to —"

"I know, David, I know. Again, let me assure you that I know you *haven't* tried anything, but the very reason I am asking you is that I know you have already been attracted to her, and, I think, she has taken to you. What I'm saying is that since you appear fond of each other, if you were to be her *paramour,* so to speak, you would be doing her a favor, and me one as well. Do you see?"

David found himself frozen in the most uncomfortable position in his chair, and felt cramps developing in both legs and in his neck, as his muscles tightened in increasing nervousness. Somehow he managed to force himself to relax slightly, and reply without appearing overly apprehensive, which in fact he was.

"Yes, I see, sir, it's just that I was afraid that you might be testing me, or something, to see if I would jump at the bait, proving that I was really interested in attempting to steal your wife." He gulped, not so discreetly this time, and tried to explain further. "I mean, not that you would lure me unfairly, of course, but if you did, you would believe it were justified. I think I'm not saying this well."

Harold Wickenham smiled warmly, and to David it appeared to be genuine. "I understand, David. You are afraid that I might be setting some sort of trap for you. Let me assure you I am not. The matter is simple. I cannot make love to my wife; my wife needs a sex life; you are a friend and are her age; she is attracted to you and you to her. The offer is simple: You may take Karen to bed, say, once a week, and have my blessing on the affair. Of course, no one would know that I approved it, not even Karen.

There it was. A license to make love to his boss's wife. And apparently Mr. Wickenham was thoroughly serious. A moment of silence passed between them, as David peered into Mr. Wickenham's eyes, and Harold Wickenham gazed coolly back, awaiting some response.

"Sir, I hope you know that this is a most unusual offer, and if I seem totally confused it's because I have never talked about something like this before. What can I say?"

"You can say yes, or no, as I see it," said Harold. "I understand it's highly irregular, and I can see why you would be flustered. Take a moment to consider it. I would want your answer now, tonight, however."

David's mind raced as he turned over the possibility, and attempted to reassure himself that Wickenham was being honest about not trying to trap him. He wondered how a thing like this would work out, whether Karen would ever find out, whether or not she would suspect that David's boldness were helped by Harold, even whether or not Karen would respond to David if and when he were to make advances toward her. In fact, how could he be certain, even having Harold's blessing, that Karen would consent to an affair, if she didn't know about the deal? Still, if she was going without the physical intimacy of marriage, and was attracted to him, and had the opportunity for a liaison, wouldn't David's romantic abilities suffice to woo her? Wickenham said he believed her to be interested in him, which confirmed what he had allowed himself to believe in the last few months.

But one other question occurred to him, and he posed it: "Forgive me, sir, but from the perspective of contract law, just what would you expect to receive as consideration?"

"Posed like the lawyer I would expect you to be. The answer is, simply the satisfaction of knowing that my wife's needs were being met. I would have no other expectations of you, whether professionally or otherwise. The conditions are simple: you would keep the matter private, not disclosing to anyone including Karen the fact of my approval or this conversation or any of its details. I would approve of your relationship, arrange times when you could accomplish, let us say, your mission, and indemnify you against any loss or penalty. If in the future I change my mind, I would agree to inform you and give you ample time, let us say, two weeks, to close out the arrangements, again without any repercussions against you in any way. Oh, and should my wife become pregnant, you would agree now to surrender any claim to fatherhood or custody of children. I would imagine, however, that you would take appropriate steps to avoid that circumstance.

David found the nervousness which had swept over him before was dissipating steadily, and as he turned over the details of the offer with his lawyer's mind, he found himself assuming that he would accept, and simply trying to work out the kinks mentally before finalizing the deal. He continued slowly and deliberately, as if stepping across a creaking and unstable floor.

"Is there a time limit on the arrangement?"

"Not as long as I continue to experience my present incapacity," said Wickenham flatly. "If that should reverse itself, I would retain the right to cancel the contract at my pleasure."

It was the strangest thing that had ever happened to David, to be sure; and the fact that it was his employer, who represented the single most powerful influence on his economic well-being at present, and on his future as well, still left him with partially weak knees. But the questions seemed to be answered, Wickenham seemed to be perfectly on the level, and it would make possible something David had daydreamed about anyway. How could he lose? He took a breath. It was now, or nothing.

"How would we memorialize the arrangement?" he asked.

"Naturally, there could be no paperwork involved in this sort of thing. I would ask you to accept my word, I would ask for yours, and we would shake hands. There can be no witnesses. That may not be ideal for a contract, but this is an unusual situation."

"That's for certain, sir," said David, lifting his eyebrows in an expression of continued amazement at what was transpiring. Then, with as much composure as he could muster, he gave his answer. "I accept."

Wickenham nodded a few times slowly, and spoke softly. "Good, good. I'm glad. It will be of benefit to us both." He came around the left side of the desk and extended his hand. "Shall we shake, then?"

David put out his hand abruptly, his unwelcome nervousness showing itself. But perhaps, after all, he should appear a bit nervous, play the part. Too cocky, too excited, and he might seem a poor sport about this. After all,

Wickenham was looking for someone to "help" him. The least David could do was to appear very servile and willing to please.

They shook twice, and released. Neither appeared to know exactly what to say next, but David realized he should ask, "You say you will make arrangements?"

"Oh, yes. Tomorrow I will be flying to New York. I will see that you have an appointment doing some field work for one of my cases, under my direction. You will be able to come here at 10:00 a.m. with the pretext of using the library for some research. You'll have as long as you like until around midnight. Every week, some day during the week, I'll let you know of arrangements for my being gone."

David nodded. Everything seemed to be taken care of. Now, how did one end a conversation of this sort, with one's boss, with the husband of his soon-to-be lover? Perhaps the simple and direct approach: "Well, good night, sir."

"We'll walk down together. Oh, take this box of cigars. They're the ones we had tonight. I brought you up here to give you something, after all."

They walked down the stairs, and reappeared in the front entrance hall, David clutching the box of cigars appreciatively, and they met Karen Wickenham coming out from the dining room.

"Well, you two, were you up there rolling those cigars by hand?" Karen said smoothly.

"No, my dear, you can't give a box of cigars by just handing them over. You have to talk about them, tell all about how you came by them, discuss the ring gauge, describe the aroma, that sort of thing. You wouldn't care, I'm sure!" Harold said playfully, and Karen shook her head in affirmation.

"You're absolutely right, and I'm glad you enjoy it," she

said. She turned to David. "Thank you for coming, David."

"I wouldn't have missed it," David managed. He started to say, 'See you tomorrow,' but caught himself in mid-thought, shook Harold's hand, and turned, going out the door. As it gently shut behind him, he shuddered suddenly, releasing the tension that had built in the past fifteen minutes, and also in anticipation of his first engagement with Karen Wickenham, in fulfillment of "the deal." What a deal, he thought. It costs me nothing, and I have a danger-free affair, ready-made, with no fear of reprisal. I must be living right, he thought. The irony and contradiction of that conclusion elicited an audible chortle, as he shut the door to his car, cruised down the driveway to the street, and headed home.

The following morning David rose at the regular time, and followed the regular routine except for a few minutes spent putting an extra touch on his hair, being more careful about applying his deodorant, and shaving just a bit closer.

Driving toward the office, his mind raced with thoughts of what the day would bring. One side of him was giddy with the expectation of seducing Karen Wickenham. But the other side of him was plagued with undefined and troubling hesitations. Even if he managed to convince Karen to enter into what was clearly an adulterous relationship with him, would it be only because Mr. Wickenham had made it possible? And what did that make David? A gigolo? A hired hand? What? It was an intellectual question, he thought to himself, and not worth interrupting his agreement with Wickenham, or his preexisting plan to attempt to start something with Wickenham's wife. An intellectual enigma, nothing more.

He arrived at the firm, entered his little cubical of an office, and was buzzed almost immediately by the shared secretary. She told him she had a file for him from Mr.

Wickenham, who said it was to help him with his research at the Wickenham estate today, and that he already knew about the assignment. David said yes, that he had already been briefed by Mr. Wickenham, and would probably be gone from shortly after nine thirty through the rest of the day.

He sat at his modest desk, browsed some papers in the file, and found himself gazing at them out of focus. He felt vaguely uneasy about the arrangement with Mr. Wickenham. Almost as if someone were looking over his shoulder and still would be, when whatever happened that day took place. Wickenham would be physically gone, of course; but David felt that whatever developed between him and Karen Wickenham would possess the character of surrogacy. Nothing had taken place yet, but already there was in his mind the gnawing sensation that he was being used. Well, he thought, if he were being used, at least he was the one who would derive the greatest pleasure from it.

Within the hour, he packed his briefcase, tossed in the file from Wickenham, left the office wearing his best professional look, and drove to Kingston Hills, pulling into the Wickenham estate at the stroke of 10:00 a.m.

Karen Wickenham opened the front door, and smiled like the sunshine itself.

"Hi, David. Harold told me you'd be coming by. Come in." She closed the door behind them. "You know where the library is. How much work did he give you?"

"I don't know yet. It may not take long at all," David said, looking for some indicator that Karen might be interested in a diversion. "Depends on how much relevant material I find."

"I'm afraid I won't be any help. I don't do law," she said playfully. A good sign.

"Sometimes, neither do I," David said laughing. He wondered if she got the hint. How was he going to go about this?

As he walked down a side hall to the library, Karen followed casually, pausing at the door, her hands on the jamb, her head resting gently on her hands, like some casual pose in a newspaper engagement photo.

"Don't work too hard," she said. "Would you like something?"

It was too easy a pun, and he avoided it. "Well, maybe some bottled water, if you have any."

"Be back in a minute," she said, sounding younger than the mature hostess of the previous evening who had greeted and entertained guests with flawless etiquette and effortless grace. In a casual setting, she appeared to be enjoying her proximity to her twenties rather than her more distant removal from her husband's fifties.

The hesitations of an hour earlier were fading somewhat in the excitement of being alone in the house with Karen Wickenham; but as she left, David glanced toward the door and was drawn to the portrait of Mr. Harold Wickenham on the wall next to the entrance. As with many portraits, the eyes of the distinguished lawyer followed the viewer around the room, and stared straight through the soul. This painting had been done no more than two years earlier, for it was an exact likeness of Wickenham in his present state, and at about a hundred and fifty percent life size, it had the imposing appearance of reality, as if the spirit of the man inhabited the room, though his body was in New York on business. David wished the open door would obscure the painting from view, but it didn't.

He set his files down on one of the large tables in the room, and scanned a shelf of some of the hundreds and hundreds of volumes lining the walls. On a small, un-shelved portion of wall directly to the right behind the desk, there was an arrangement of plaques, awards, and honorary certificates, surrounding a commemorative issue of a WWII 45 caliber pistol. Underneath were several decanters with spirits. For a moment David entertained the idea of pouring himself something stiffer than flavored water.

But shortly, Karen returned, with two bottles, one for him and one, he presumed, for her. She sat down on the leather couch underneath the window overlooking the back acreage. The brilliant morning light created a halo around her blond hair, which this morning she wore down and flowing around her shoulders, instead of up as she had the previous evening. She looked particularly alluring. David was certain it was intentional.

"I won't bother you here, will I?" said Karen?

"No, not at all," David replied. "It will be nice to have some company. A lot of this work is dull and boring. I thought so in law school, and I still do."

David spent a few minutes pulling various volumes out of shelves around the room, referring to sheets of paper in his hand, and then he carried them to one of the work tables, the one nearest Karen, where he could be conveniently distracted by her. After another five minutes or so, he looked up, to find her turning up her bottle of raspberry flavored water and taking a slow, sensuous sip, before lowering it, and wiping a small drop from her bottom lip with her little finger.

*A scene-board clapped noisily in front of the eyes of his mind, between him and Karen, as an imaginary cinematographer called, "Action." David, playing David, rose slowly, and strode over to Karen, sat, with one leg folded under him, beside her on the leather couch, put a finger under her chin, prompting her to lean up to his lips. They kissed softly. "Cut!" the director said,* and David came back into focus on Karen's eyes, which now appeared not to be focused on him but distractedly on the far wall, where the picture of her husband peered down at them with a slight hint of disapproval.

*"Take two," said the director, "a-n-d action!" David turned back to Karen. "Karen," he said, "look at me." She did so, and exuded passion. " I've wanted you to look at me like that for so long," he said. They rose simultaneously and hesitantly, then moved toward each other, meeting and embracing all in one sweeping movement, their limbs entwined in a sudden burst of unveiled ardor. As they broke from their kiss briefly, she looked over his shoulder and saw Harold Wickenham come in the door.*

*"Harold!" she called, and David whirled around.*

*"Mr. Wickenham!" said David. But Wickenham sat down in a side chair facing them, as if settling into a theater seat for a show.*

*"Don't mind me. Go ahead. Nothing I like more than to see my wife having a good time," he said, and added, "And remember, David, you're doing this for me."*

*"Cut," called the director. "Mr. Wickenham, I would prefer your not being in this scene."*

David felt the same way, as he looked at Karen Wickenham on the couch, gazing past him to the wall, obviously daydreaming, as he was, maddeningly, or else she was engaged in idle thoughts about nothing. How was he going to go about this?

He tried to follow her gaze. Actually, she was looking more in the direction of the first shelf past the painting, where general reference books were located, including several translations of the Bible. Great, thought David, more encouraging influences. Then again, he mused, the Bible contained many interesting and earthy stories about lust and sex. In fact, the biblical David made a little time in his time.

The name of Bathsheba came to him from childhood church experiences. So did a sketchy outline of the rest of the story, which present-day David realized went on to say that the biblical David lived to regret his lust, which everybody found out about, and which ended with a man murdered, and a baby who died.

David tried to expurgate not only the story but the Bible from his mind altogether, but before he could, another story came to mind. It was Sarah, wife of Abraham, offering him her handmaiden, Hagar, since Sarah didn't seem to be able to have children. Abraham, David seemed to remember, appreciated the arrangement (for the holiest of reasons, of course), and carried it out with enthusiasm, but things went downhill after that. Something about sibling rivalry, and Abraham having to listen to the wives squabble, wishing he had never agreed to surrogate sex.

David looked back around at Karen. She was reading the label on the water bottle, and alternately gazing out the window distractedly, as out on the back lawn the sounds of two large dogs, yapping in a kennel, wafted in.

*"Action!" called the director. David got up, being led to do so by a gentle prod from a leather leash around his neck, which extended up out of sight, disappearing into a fog above him. He was brought around to the couch, where he saw Karen looking up at him, lips parted, panting. A voice from above him commanded him, "Mate! boy, Mate!"*

*Say "cut!" said David to the director.*

This is insane. Why am I here? As his eyes came back into focus, he looked back at Karen, who was still staring with lazy boredom out the window. He looked over to the portrait on the wall. There was Wickenham, wearing a slight, mocking smile. He seemed to be daring him to act. For his own part,

David could not figure out how he would act if he wanted to, which he did, he thought, or had thought the day before. Suddenly though, in twenty-four hours, the thought of seducing Karen Wickenham had turned sour. She wasn't aware of the "agreement," he knew, not only because Harold had said he would not tell her, but also because she gave no indication that she knew. If she had, and had agreed to the plan, certainly she would have divulged it, or made some move toward David. Plainly, she didn't know, and that was making things even harder for David, because he had to figure out a way to interest her in an affair when she had many a reason to stay far away from anything that hinted of immorality.

Immorality. Why did David think of that? Not that he didn't realize in his mind, somewhere in the back corner of it, that an affair was immoral. Just that he wondered why, right now, as he was trying to plan an affair, he was reminding himself of how wrong it was.

Wrong. Heck, that didn't bother him half so much just now as the fact that having an affair with Karen Wickenham, even if he could convince her, was like being a stand in for her husband. He couldn't imagine that he would be able to get Harold Wickenham out of his mind even if he were able to get Karen Wickenham into the bedroom. Cheap, that's what it was. He felt cheap, bought. He felt as if he were a male prostitute. And he hadn't even done anything!

Perhaps these were just the predictable jitters to go along with something as unusual as this arrangement. Perhaps another day or so of getting used to the idea would find his attitude ameliorated. Somehow he didn't think so. But maybe today wasn't the best of days to begin the affair in earnest. He had to have time to think the thing through more thoroughly.

Another glance at Karen, who was not paying him any attention at all, convinced him to wait. Something about this entire deal was sour. He would finish the research and leave. No excuse would be necessary, would it, since as far as Karen knew he had only come there to use the library after all?

David turned back to his work. There was just one more citation to summarize. The State vs. Kaltman, 1964. Kaltman was an attorney charged with murder. Hmm. David scanned the technical jargon and got to the meat of the case. His eyes began to widen. It seems that Kaltman was the senior partner in the law firm of Kaltman, O'Brien and Fisher. One evening in 1963, Kaltman arrived home early from a business trip to find Fisher at his home, in a compromising position with Kaltman's wife, Anne. Kaltman flew into a rage, understandably, grabbed what everyone thought was a non-working replica of a pistol from his wall, and shot Fisher before he could even don a robe and launch into an explanation of what he was doing there, which seemed at the moment to be altogether too obvious. Fisher died in the hospital. Kaltman was charged with murder, but under the state's provision for extenuating circumstances in such cases, and obviously in sympathy with Kaltman's righteous indignation, the jury found him not guity.

David was pale. He could see the veins in his wrist pumping at a pulse rate of a hundred or more. His eyebrows began to drip with perspiration. He felt sick at his stomach. Harold Wickenham seemed to be laughing from the portrait on the wall. Karen Wickenham, who looked like a luscious dessert a few minutes before, looked like a human mousetrap, as she sat in the window sill, now, sipping her raspberry water.

David shut the book, and gathered his papers together, doing his dead level best to avoid shaking. Karen turned to see him rising.

"Are you finished?" she asked.

"Entirely," he said. "There wasn't much to do, just as I thought. I have to go. Thanks for the water. And, uh, do you mind if I leave the books here on the table? I really have to hurry." It occurred to David that if Wickenham were planning to return home unexpectedly, he would like very much to miss him, even if he wouldn't have found the two of them in a 'compromising position.' And never would, he thought. Wickenham must be a madman, luring him this way, trapping him. What sort of maniacal diversion was he playing at?

"I'm sure Harold won't mind," she said about the books. David was already out the door and midway down the hall. She followed him, wondering at his haste, and watched him dart to the front door, hastily make his exit, and roar away, wasting gas. She shrugged, turned up the last of her water, finished shutting the door David had left ajar, and retreated to her sitting room to read a good book.

David passed the turnoff to his apartment, and continued down the boulevard to the freeway, cruising at just over the maximum allowable speed as a therapy for his frustration, fear and anger. The deal was definitely off. He would step into Wickenham's office the next morning, tell him that he had patched up things with a former girlfriend, and that he wouldn't feel right about cheating on her, and that he was sure Mr. Wickenham would understand. In passing, he would also claim that he had not been able to complete his research, which would suggest to Wickenham that he had not seen the threatening case study. The explanation would surely work;

it would get him off the hook, and off the leash. Wickenham may have had some sadistic plan to entrap him, but Mrs. Harold Wickenham would never be David's mistress, you could bet on that.

That evening at 11:15 p.m. Harold Wickenham opened the front door, stepped in, put down his briefcase, locked the door behind him, and carried his flight bag upstairs to the bedroom. Karen Wickenham was already in bed, sitting up finishing the last chapter of her romance novel.

"Hi, sweetie," cooed Karen.

"Hi, hon," said Harold.

"Tough trip?"

"Not really," he said, as he slipped out of his suit, baring a still-toned, fifty-ish body. "It's gotten to be routine. I have to make this trip every once in a while to straighten out a recurring situation. I have it down to a science, now." Disrobed now down to a pair of deep green silk shorts, Harold sauntered over to the bed. "How about a welcome-home gift?"

"Oh!" she said playfully. "For me, or *from* me?"

"How about both?" said Harold.

Karen closed the book around a marker, set it on the bedside table, lifted the sheet and said coyly, "Come on in, lover."

Harold dimmed the light, slid in beside his gracious and lovely wife, more than twenty years his junior, and Mr. and Mrs. Wickenham enjoyed themselves in each others arms as they did thrice weekly, and sometimes more.

# The Remote

He really didn't like to admit it, but Jack Logan was a couch potato. It wasn't that he had planned it. In fact, having remarked in recent years that his father had always been a couch potato, even before the term was coined somewhere in the late eighties, Jack had most definitely planned *not* to be glued to the couch.

Of course, he really didn't sit on the couch. He had a leather recliner, extra wide, with deep padding on the leg rest, accessory pillows to cradle his waist and support his back, and a special pillow his wife had made for his neck, that prevented stiffness in the event that he went to sleep in the chair, which he rarely did. A mere technicality. He was still a couch potato. From the time he returned from work at 5:30 until midnight or better, he was firmly ensconced in his chair in front of his 103" plasma screen and the wall-long entertainment center underneath it, except for a brief stint at the supper table, or short trips to reload the CD/DVD multi-changer, if he didn't simply switch to a streaming feed to watch something online.

Jack wasn't a dull boy by any means. He was a person fascinated with many things, an educated man who had a smattering of knowledge about dozens of specialized areas, who prided himself on being something of a modern renaissance man. He could converse on just about any topic with what he believed to be better-than-average expertise, only sometimes talking out of school. Television viewing added to his knowledge since he watched all the major PBS, NatGeo, History Channel and Discovery Channel specials, and constantly scanned CNN, Fox and other news services.

But couch potato he was, and one of his greatest fascinations of all was electronic gadgetry. Like many men his age, he had one, childhood foot in the pre-PC world of books and analogical devices, and the other foot in cyberspace. He understood computer technology at least as well if not better than his kids, who thought they understood everything. But having seen computers sweep the culture and miraculously replace or augment seemingly everything in their path from clocks to cars, he was permanently fascinated with how they did what they did, and devoted to acquiring (within reason) every new consumer device that came out.

His home was fully wired for computer controls. A security system capable of full controlling by voice recognition had been installed three months ago. Most lights and appliances were hooked into a timing and voltage monitoring device that made everything from remote control of the oven to programmable operation of lights and sound systems as easy as punching numbers on a telephone keypad or with an app on his iPhone or iPad, which, by the way, one could do long distance from a vacation hotel.

Every Friday, when Jack left his office at Forrester Public Relations Associates, he went the long way home, down Adams Blvd. by all the consumer electronics stores, and stopped in two or three just to browse, keeping his mental database up to date on the latest technological must-haves. This Friday, he chose Larry's Lectronics Lair, a small operation that had opened up during the previous year, specializing in DVDs, Blu-Rays, digital video and audio players, surround sound stereos with all the bells and whistles, and the gizmos that controlled them all from the couch—or, in Jack's case, the recliner.

The Lair was buzzing with activity, mostly in the sound room, when Jack went in. Larry, the quiet but clearly brilliant young man who owned the little store was waiting on a woman who didn't know what she wanted exactly, just that it was for her son and that it played MP3s "really loud." Larry looked up, tilted his head up in recognition of Jack's entry and continued patiently trying to help the woman settle on something.

Jack busied himself with an ultra-compact video camera that docked into a small, full featured editing unit or plugged into a laptop for production. Cool!

Momentarily Larry extracted himself from the confused woman, who continued to touch displayed stereos and mutter to herself. He came over to Jack, shook his hand, and introduced himself.

"Hi. I'm Larry Wilson. Welcome to Larry's Lair. Been here before?"

"No," said Jack, "I pass by every day, and I watched as the store went up. It was just a matter of time, though—I'm an electronics nut."

"Great! We like nuts here," Larry quipped. "What kind of thing interests you most?"

"Gadgets, without any question," Jack said proudly. If it beeps, lights up, shoots a beam, controls a box, I like it and I want one!"

Larry grinned and nodded, and looked Jack in the eye. "I have something you don't have, yet." There was a little glint in his eye, like a secret sign from one conspirator to another. Good salesmen worked hard to fake the look, because every customer liked to think he was getting an inside deal on an exclusive product.

"Yeah?" said Jack, beginning to salivate. "What is it?"

"It's an experimental product, not on the general market yet," explained Larry in a low voice. "I have only one. It's one of about a dozen prototype units."

"What does it do?" Jack pressed him.

"It's a remote."

"Just a remote?"

"No, not just a remote." Larry led him along gradually, releasing tidbits at a tantalizing rate. "It's a multi-function remote to begin with, like some others. Controls up to three TVs or screens, four video sources, miscellaneous boxes, and a single program-ready stereo system, like the new ComVox."

Jack's eyes lit up. "That's considerably more than most multi-function controllers do."

"Yes, it is," admitted Larry. "And it would be worth it to have this little toy even if that were all it would do. But it has several other features you will find interesting."

"I'm listening. Sell me!" Jack said.

"First of all, it is voice controllable. You can program it to respond to your voice alone, or to several voices. You can give it detailed instructions by voice or by the keypad to turn systems on or off at given times. There's an LCD display that gives you status reports on all activated units. There are several other things that are listed in the manual"— Larry reached into his back pocket and gave Jack a pocket-sized but fairly thick manual, offset printed and bound imprecisely with nondescript materials—"and I've been told that there are some undocumented features that people who aren't afraid to experiment will be able to find for themselves."

Larry pointed toward a shelf in the back corner of the little shop, and led Jack over to it. Reaching into a glass-doored recess he pulled out an oversized remote control unit, about eleven inches long, three inches wide, and nearly an inch thick. On top were several banks of keys. On the bottom of the controller face was a bank of buttons most of which looked like they related to a stereo system or television. In the middle was a dial, with an indentation for a fingertip, which looked as if it could control volume. Around it were some colored but unlabeled buttons that had universal symbols, Jack supposed, though like some symbols on car dashboards, they weren't as universal or immediately recognizable as they were supposed to be. Near the top or front of the unit was a recognizable array of video source control buttons, a number pad, and function and enter-keys, some color coded. And at the very front of the unit, instead of a deep red or amber lens where the signal emitted, was instead a small dome, positioned on the face. It was semi-spherical, about the diameter of a dime, and made out of transparent but darkly tinted acrylic material.

"What's the little dome for? Three-sixty signal dispersion?" Jack asked knowledgeably.

"Exactly," nodded Larry. "You can be anywhere in the room, and not pointing the remote at all, and it will still work. In fact, it uses a new technology. The signals will bounce off ceilings and walls generally, which makes it work even when there are obstacles between you and the entertainment center."

Jack was enthralled. For a moment he just stared at the unit, taking in its face plate, absorbing the overall impact of the piece. It had a kind of cybernetic lure to it, as if somewhere in the maze of buttons, symbols and cryptic abbreviations there were a subliminal message mesmerizing him.

*The Remote*

Larry stood motionless, allowing the gadget to sell itself. He knew Jack was going to buy the device before he left the store. Some customers looked a thing over a dozen times before returning the thirteenth to purchase it. Jack may have done so before, but Larry could tell an instant sale when he saw one, and Jack was smitten beyond his ability to resist.

"This is awesome," said Jack. He turned the remote over, inspected the battery compartment, which like the unit itself was oversized, and concluded it took six or maybe eight batteries. Removing the sliding door, he found space for eight, plus two silver oxide-type batteries.

"Takes a lot of power" he said.

"Works at a greater distance. Mostly, though, the added voltage is for the extra features. Apparently, they eat up amps big time. There's a lithium ion power pack you can get instead, if you want, but it's expensive. Load her up with alkalines and go." Larry smiled confidently, while Jack replaced the door, brushing off his fingerprints, as if the remote were some jewel or piece of polished gold.

Jack turned the remote back over, and looked up. "Have you used it?" he asked.

"No. Actually, I've been hoping to find somebody interested in giving it some beta testing, reporting to me on how it works. The company wants consumer feedback before marketing it widely. Whoever buys it will get a pretty hefty rebate when he reports on it." Not too subtle, Larry realized, but Jack was probably beyond noticing the sales technique.

Jack looked back down at the remote, and back up at Larry. "How much is it?"

"It's $200.00. I know—that's a lot for the average remote, but the rebate is a hundred fifty, so it's not like you won't get most of it back for being a beta tester."

Jack reached into his pocket, opened his wallet, looked briefly, and reported his findings: "I'm your man."

Larry grinned excitedly. "I'll get the box. And it has a little padded leather case, too." He disappeared into the back room, and emerged in less than a minute with a dark brown pouch, and an unmarked box that held the bagged remote snugly. Larry took the remote, went over to an accessory counter, quickly popped open some battery packages, and loaded the remote with the proper power source.

"I'm throwing in the batteries no cost," he said casually. Then he put the remote in the pouch, put the pouch into the box, and presented it to Jack.

Jack pulled out two crisp hundred dollar bills and put them in Larry's hand. Larry got Jack's address and phone number for record keeping, then scribbled out a sales slip. Promising to give Larry some sort of progress report by Monday morning, Jack carried his precious, small cargo out the door of the shop, slid into his vehicle, expressing no interest in any more gadget hunting this Friday, and motored home with more satisfaction and anticipation than he had experienced in months.

When he walked in the back door of his house, his wife Ellen was on the cordless phone, the receiver between her chin and shoulder, as she talked while tending something on the stove. She had a bluetooth ear set for her cell phone but she wouldn't use it. She thought they were pretentious. If it were up to her, she would still be using a rotary phone, but Jack had accidentally-on-purpose broken the last of those dinosaurs that had hung on the kitchen wall several years ago. Ellen waved with her eyebrows as Jack passed behind her and sniffed at supper.

His son Jeff came down the hall, passed by the kitchen

door, hailed Jack with a "hi, dad" as he disappeared, and could be heard bounding down the stairs to the basement-recreation room where he and his sister Nia had all their toys and created worlds of their own.

Jack moved into the den, took out his new toy, hefted it, sat down in his chair, and rearranged the items on the chair-side table to accommodate the new controller. That meant first removing two other controllers, which he felt certain he would be able to store away permanently once he had figured out how to use the new one. He looked over his right shoulder through the pass-through that connected the den to the kitchen area. He could see Ellen, and she was still on the phone. Jack thought he would like to experiment a few minutes with the remote before he told anybody about it.

He opened the thick manual, fanned its pages, located a section on TV and stopped. Instructions were there on how to program the remote by depressing a button and waiting for the television to respond. The remote then auto-programmed. When a green light flashed indicating success, Jack then pointed the remote, thought about it, pointed it in the opposite direction, and pressed "on." The television turned on dutifully, tuned to CNN. A quick check of the number pad, up and down keys, and volume adjustment showed Jack that the unit worked perfectly.

In a few minutes Jack had found the corresponding controls for his CD, DVD, Blu-Ray, MP3 unit, and every other unit plugged into his sound and video systems. He started the playback on the DVD recorder, which had a movie he had recorded during the wee hours of Thursday night. It was a thriller, loaded with bombings, knifings and other gory fare. Jack turned down the volume and let it run, and began looking over the remote for reasonable key presses to turn on the stereo system, which had its own remote, now stacked with the others out of sight. On the middle bank of buttons, there were several marked with what looked like indications of frequency control, tone adjustment and various other stereo-related subjects. But on the left side of the unit, beside the little volume dial, was an unmarked, amber-colored button. Pressing it, Jack looked up at the entertainment center, scanning the displays and listening critically to volume and tone. The button, however, had no visible or audible result. Jack held the unit up just to make certain, or just because it's what often was the cause of malfunctioning buttons with other, less sophisticated remotes, and he pressed the button again. Still the amber button didn't function.

Perhaps it functioned like the "alt" key on a computer. Jack held the unit in his left hand, reached over with his left thumb and pushed the amber button down, then looked for a reasonable button to push in combination with it. Since the cable movie was running, Jack found the "pause" button, and pressed it firmly.

At first it was difficult to tell what had happened. The DVD had not paused, exactly, but appeared to have shut off, though it hadn't cycled through its shut-down phase in the usual way, but stopped abruptly as if having been disconnected, though the display still indicated it was on. The television was lit up, but fuzz filled the screen. Otherwise, the Alt-pause button combination seemed to have had no useful effect.

After Jack had breathed in and out twice more, however, and clearly heard himself doing it, he realized that ambient room sounds had all but ceased. He looked up. He was the only one in the room, of course, and nothing had been making noise anyway; but he suddenly became aware of the dead stillness of everything. His cat Sierra had been reclining on the sofa when he came in, and was not asleep, but sitting with all fours tucked in underneath him, watching Jack like the sphinx. He was still looking toward Jack, but was as motionless as a pyramid. Jack flinched. The cat didn't.

Then Jack noticed that the clock on the wall above the sofa was not ticking. Looking at his watch, he saw that the wall clock showed approximately the right time, but it was quickly getting behind, because it had apparently just stopped the moment before. The television and DVD continued to run. But things in the room that had been moving physically had stopped. In a moment of eerie realization, Jack became aware that he no longer heard sounds from behind him in the kitchen. Afraid, but urgent to know, he leaned out and around the right side of the chair and peered toward the pass-through to the kitchen. On the other side, facing the counter, her waist to shoulders visible to him, was Ellen. She was stirring something into a pan of sauce. Or, she had been. At the moment, all spoon clinking was silenced, as her hand held the spoon motionless in the pan, amid stirring. Her right hand held a spice jar of some kind, as if she were keeping it still to read the label. But there was no motion, no motion at all. In fact, she wasn't even breathing. Whipping around quickly, Jack studied the cat carefully. The cat wasn't breathing either.

Surely the remote hadn't done this—that was crazy—but how could it have been anything else? And suppose it had. What would happen to his wife, and the cat? How long had it been since he had pushed the button? A minute? More perhaps? Was he endangering their lives by having stopped their motion, including their breathing? A wave of panic came over him, and Jack fumbled with the remote. He held the amber button down and quickly depressed the pause button as well.

Immediately, the low, white noise of moving air, moving bodies, and ticking clocks resumed. The spoon clinked in the pan, and as he turned around to see his wife, he could detect nothing different in her movements, no sign that she was out of breath or even thought that anything had happened. Sierra the cat was staring at him, blinking occasionally, and yawning once grandly. The clock was keeping perfect time, but had fallen behind his watch by about a minute and a half. The DVD had resumed, without going through its load and play cycle. Everything was back to normal.

Sitting there trying to take it all in, Jack found himself trembling. In fact, he was suddenly overcome with a wave of fear, not the kind one has when faced with great danger, but the kind experienced after a harrowing incident when he realizes he could have been killed and wasn't. It had only now caught up with him what he had done. Simply pressing keys on a remote control unit had stopped the world, and he had gotten away with it.

The very thought of such a thing was ludicrous, and he nearly cackled out loud thinking it, but that's what had happened. It occurred to him to consider that this may have been one of those rare occasions when Jack fell asleep in his chair, and that he might be dreaming all the foregoing moments. Somewhere he had learned that you can't really pinch yourself when you're dreaming, so he didn't try it, but it did cross his mind that if he was not, in fact dreaming, he might be able to repeat his actions and make everything stop again.

Without thinking it through as much as he knew he

should, he touched the two buttons again. Instantly, every motion in the room ceased, and the dead calm that had prevailed during the last pause reigned again over the room. Ellen's spoon fell silent. The cat was in the middle of biting at some critter in his fur along his right side, and looked like a bird sleeping with its head buried under its wing. The clock was stopped. As before, however, his watch was running, the second hand ticking away unaffected.

Why was his watch running? In fact, why was the television still on, albeit displaying fuzz? Logical wheels began to turn. All motion was stopped. But his watch was digital. The television was, of course, electronic. The DVD clock display, which was on, was digital. The mechanical, moving parts had stopped, but electronics continued, since nothing in them—at least nothing larger than the electrons in the circuits—was moving. It appeared that the remote, whatever powers it had, whatever signal it put out, was interrupting the motion of physical things, but not at an atomic or molecular level.

Jack got up slowly, as if moving normally would break the spell. That's what it was like: a spell cast on everything around him. He almost tiptoed as he walked into the quiet kitchen. He had to look at Ellen up close. She was standing at the counter, her back to the center of the kitchen, but sideways to him. She would have seen him if she hadn't been "paused." From the first pause, he was fairly certain she was not aware of anything during the extended moment of the phenomenon.

Jack walked over to her and looked at what she was doing. She was pouring sauce from the pan into a casserole dish, but it was "frozen" in space—not that it was by any means cold, for steam was rising from it. Rather, steam had been rising from it and was now hanging in the air like a cloud, motionless. Jack wondered if the sauce was hot to the touch, or would feel like one of those rubber things made to look like vomit. He decided not to touch it.

He leaned over and slowly moved as far in front of Ellen as he could, right in her face. Her eyes were not dilated, as a dead person's would be, but they were as fixed. There was no hint of breath, no pulse, nothing. He touched her sweater. The fabric moved under his fingertip. It seemed he could move things, but they were not moving of their own. Nothing was.

Why, then, was Jack himself still moving? He was the closest thing to the remote, but it hadn't affected him at all. Perhaps he was "grounded," in some way by holding the remote. It made sense. Why would someone design something that could manipulate time, or at least motion, but would incapacitate the operator? That was it: the operator was grounded.

What didn't make sense was that something, *anything,* especially something so small, could control the movement of the world. But he had just made that part up, hadn't he? He didn't know what was affected besides the kitchen and the den of his own house. How far did the effect go? It embarrassed him to think that he had concluded that a little remote control had stopped the world.

He stopped to listen carefully. From here in the kitchen, closer to the hall, he suddenly realized there were sounds indicating motion elsewhere in the house. Through the hall door to the basement recreation room came the muffled tones of Jeff's voice, dictating some make-believe game to Nia. They were unaffected. Just then, Jack became aware of the noise of a passing car on the street in front of their house.

That pretty well narrowed it down to the vicinity of the den and kitchen, the area that might be expected to be affected by the signal from a normal remote control. That was a relief really, because it meant that he was manipulating time or motion only in his own house.

It had been nearly five minutes since Jack had pressed the amazing pause button. He felt he should return things to normal. He decided not to return to the chair, however. Backing up a step or two from his wife, he stood behind her, in the center of the kitchen. His grip firm on the remote, he pressed the two buttons. Ellen recommenced her spatula motions and the sauce poured and the steam resumed rising, as the DVD picked up where it had left off in the den. As Jack waited motionlessly behind her, Ellen finished emptying the contents of the bowl and turned toward the sink.

"Oh! I didn't see you come in—how did you get there so quietly? Would you get the butter out of the fridge, please?" It was all one statement-question rolled together, and luckily no answer was needed to her wonderment. Jack opened the refrigerator with his right hand, held it open with his knee, and retrieved the butter. As he handed it to Ellen, she noticed the remote in his left hand.

"What's that thing?" she asked.

"It's a new remote for the entertainment center," Jack said as casually as he could manage.

"Another one? We already have two—what do we need another one for, for pity's sake?"

"This one will replace the other two. It'll make things simpler." That was possibly true, but in all probability, the original remotes were much simpler, if only because they had fewer buttons among which to find the one you wanted. But in view of what Larry had called the "undocumented features" of the remote, appealing to its simple operation of the TV and DVD was all Jack wanted to mention at this point.

Ellen went into the hall and called Jeff and Nia up from the basement to set the table and get washed up for supper. Jack went back into the den and used the remote, normally this time, to change to a local news station, then sat down. He flipped through the remote's manual once again, looking for headings that might hint at any of the unit's unbelievable capabilities. Nothing. He had owned software for his laptop that had undocumented features, like shortcut keystrokes and the like. But this! This was a major function. Jack wondered if in fact this was an intended feature, not documented simply because it was too dangerous or fantastic, or if it were perhaps an anomaly, a mistake, something even the inventor didn't know about. How could that be? Surely a function like this couldn't happen just by accident; yet, he couldn't understand how it could happen at all. What kind of signal or beam could stop people and physical motion in their tracks?

He was staring at the face of the remote. Why it hadn't occurred to him before now he didn't know, but the question was obvious: if Alt-pause made things stop, would Alt-FF make them go fast-forward? Would Alt-Rew make them go backward? The possibilities were devilish, and Jack found himself thinking of some outlandish examples.

There was no time like the present to give it a try. Jack got up, stood where he could see Ellen's movement in the kitchen, and readied the remote. He depressed the amber key, and then located the rewind key that was grouped with the pause key. While he watched Ellen, he pushed it firmly.

Ellen slowed quickly to a stop in front of the stove, as she was picking up the finished casserole. She lingered there, as the house grew silent. Then she started moving again, slowly at first, then at a normal speed, but entirely in reverse. She put down the dish with a strange awkwardness, and seemed to deal the pot holders like cards to the counter beside the stove. Walking backward, her hands went to her waist in front, and her apron flew to them and she began wiping them. She almost backed into the opposite counter, then whipped around to face it, picked up some utensils, and appeared to put them in the drawer to her right.

It was fascinating to watch. On the stove the steam came out of the air and sank into the casserole. Ellen backed up to the sink, and turned to face it. In a moment, she backed away from the sink, and continued through the hall door. She was going to the basement door. Jack would have followed her, but quickly he thought to himself that if she were moving, it was likely that he would be visible to her, and she might perceive *his* motion as backwards instead of hers, and would later question him about it. He decided to remain frozen in place in his vantage point.

Ellen disappeared into the hall for about three seconds, then Jack heard her say something. "rpus uht pumuk oot ooy," it sounded like. She was calling Jeff and Nia up to supper.

Suddenly Jack realized that if Nia and Jeff were not going backwards, they would hear her speaking backwards and think mom had flipped. He looked down at the remote quickly and wondered what to do. If the DVD went into review mode by pressing "Rew" while in the play mode, and went back to normal by pressing play again, then Alt-Play must cancel Alt-Rew. Hastily he pressed the two keys. House sounds died down, then began again, and in two seconds

Ellen called out, "You two come up to supper!" In another three seconds, she came through the door, went to the sink briefly, turned and went to the cabinet, took out silverware, put it on the cabinet, turned and went to the stove, wiping her hands and dropping the apron just before arriving at the stove, where she picked up pot holders and began to lift the casserole dish.

This was incredible. Again, the remote had controlled physical actions, but Ellen was unaware that she had gone backwards and then repeated her previous movements. Jack stood in amazement.

Fast forward probably had the predictably opposite effect. He started to try it, and then realized that if Jeff and Nia came up at this moment, they would see a very strange sight. Better to wait until everybody was in the room.

Jack went back to his chair, and put the remote down on the table. Then he picked it up again and put it in the cabinet below. Momentarily he got up again and went to the supper table. After supper, he was going to have some real fun!

All during the meal, Jack found himself on the edge of laughter, incredulous of the phenomenal power of the remote. Ellen looked at him curiously, detecting his barely concealed smirk.

Conversation during dinner was predictable. The kids bickered over something asinine, Ellen complained about her job, and Jack replied "Hmm" at the appropriate places, occasionally requesting his children to desist. When everyone had finished, plates were stacked up in the kitchen, and Jeff and Nia bounded out of the area hoping not to be caught for KP before they had managed to get out of earshot. They were not successful, however, as Ellen had long since learned this routine, and called their names with her back turned, before they even managed to make it through the kitchen.

"Aw, Mom," Nia protested, "we did the dishes last night!"

"Yeah, and the night before," added Jeff. They both skulked back into the kitchen, trudging heavily to show their displeasure. Ellen harped at them in a motherly way, but with the edge of a woman who has 'had it up to here,' and she began to lose her temper as they tried to argue her out of making them help clean up.

Meanwhile, Jack had moved over to the den cabinet. Retrieving the remote, he stood watching the battle taking place in the kitchen, and thinking how many times he had listened to them squabble, their voices increasing in volume as their arguments decreased in logic. Many a time he had wished he could simply call it to a halt with a command or a look. Years ago he seemed to have had that capacity, but he had long ago lost the respect or the tone of authority, or something, and it didn't work anymore just to raise his voice and tell them to stop. But as fate would have it, in his hands was a technological replacement for respect. Fate, or something else.

His left thumb on the 'Alt' button and his right index on 'pause,' Jack calmly pressed them together. Jeff was frozen with a sullen mask, and Nia had her head tilted to one side, her eyebrows furrowed, her mouth open in a suspended complaint. Ellen, hands on hips, glared at them both with resolve mixed with frustration. The three of them were a monument to discord.

Jack stared at them with satisfaction. Of course, he couldn't leave them like that, though part of him really wished he could. But while they were paused, time went on in the rest of the world. If they were interrupted for a long enough interval, they would surely miss the time. That thought reminded Jack that he would have to reset the affected clocks when no one was looking.

Reluctantly, Jack un-paused them. The argument continued. Jeff banged pans "accidentally" in protest, Nia continued sniping, and Ellen issued commands to quit complaining and just do the work.

Jack suddenly realized there was more than one way to skin the proverbial cat, and fingered the Alt-FF buttons. Ellen began to skitter back and forth across the kitchen floor, the children breezed through the dishes, the clinking pans and plates sounding like the rattle of a snare drum. Every second's motion was probably the equivalent of ten seconds in normal time. When they had wiped their hands dry and raced out the door, and Ellen had turned off the sink light, Jack un-paused them. The house returned to silence.

Ellen made her way over into the den area and flopped into the corner of the couch. She began to recite the various difficulties she had experienced during the day. To Jack it was a verbal collage of discordant colors, strung together in a theme of grumbling. It was stream-of-consciousness griping, like a cheap, shallow version of Proust.

Jack found himself listening in brief segments, between his own thoughts. Almost without thinking, he pressed Alt-FF again. Ellen's gestures sped up many times over normal, and her mouth fluttered away. What sounds she was making were both muted and compressed, and quickly became white noise. He glanced at her now and then, just to check her progress. It only mildly concerned him that she may have asked him something during her diatribe. When she appeared to be giving it a rest, he canceled the effect.

She was staring at him in an odd way. "Well?" she said. Apparently she had, indeed, posed a question. He looked at her blankly. "You weren't even listening to me, were you?" she said.

"Yes, I was," he lied. "I'm thinking."

"So what's to think about? Do you or don't you?"

"Uh, I don't know," Jack said, stalling, while he reached for the remote. Pushing Alt-Rew, he watched while Ellen stared at him motionlessly, then backed into her lengthy speech. When she appeared briefly to have a quizzical look on her face, and to be looking directly at him, he waited a beat, then restored her.

Ellen continued as before, only now at normal speed. "And mother wants us to come see her next weekend. I told her we could. Do you have a problem with that?"

Uncertain whether or not he was obliged to repeat his own remarks, or if Ellen were experiencing some sort of deja-vu at this point, Jack took the shortest route and simply answered her. "No, no problem," he said, bored. And Ellen shut up, picked up a magazine, and began to absorb herself.

Presently, Jack put the remote down by the far side of the chair, next to the wall where it was out of view, and got up, mumbling that he had to make a trip to the bathroom. When he had gone down the hall and had shut the bathroom door, he heard the phone chirp. Back in the den, the cordless was by Ellen on the end table, and she picked it up.

"Hello? Yes he is . . . uh, but he's tied up right now. Can I give him a message?" The man on the other end of the line began relaying a short message. "Go ahead," said Ellen, "Okay, this is Gary, did you say? Oh, Larry? Okay, go ahead. Yes, he showed it to me. It what? What sort of problem? Can you describe it? Maybe you'd better tell him. I can have him call you back in just a few minutes. What's the number?" She wrote down the digits. "I'll have him call you. Thank you.

Bye." Ellen put down the phone and went back to the magazine.

It was about ten minutes before Jack came back into the den. He flopped back into his custom chair, and reached for the remote. Using its normal mode, he turned on the television. Ellen looked up, saw him switch on the set, which reminded her of the message.

"Oh, the phone was for you," she said, "and I told the man I would have you call back. I didn't understand exactly what he was saying. It was Larry? Larry at the electronics store? Do you know him?"

Jack sat up in the chair. Why would Larry call him? "What did he say," Jack asked warily.

"Something about the remote control you just bought. He said he had just gotten in a product notice about it, something about a warning from the factory, about some button you push that may have unpredictable results. He asked if you were having fun playing with it. What did he mean by that, Jack?"

Jack felt nervous perspiration cooling his upper lip. He didn't want Ellen to know anything about the remote's "undocumented" features. Why did the phone have to ring while he was in the bathroom? Now Ellen was asking questions. And she was not the sort to be waved off with a casual, dismissive answer to her queries. She was like one of those yellow journalists on the TV news-magazine shows, who with their cameramen run down streets, stick feet in doors, shove microphones into men's faces and demand what they have to say about rumors that they've been seen sleeping with other people's wives or have been embezzling money. He could say, "I don't know what he's talking about," but she would know he was lying, and would press him until she got some sort of believable answer, and that would undoubtedly have to be the truth, because he seldom got away with lying to her.

Nevertheless, he gave it a try. "I don't know. Did he leave the number?"

"Here it is." Ellen reached out to him with the note. "What did he mean about playing with it?" Jack nodded very slightly to himself. He was right, wasn't he. She wouldn't give it up. He didn't take the note just yet.

"You know, work it, operate it, play with it. It's a gadget. It's supposed to be fun to use."

"That's not what it sounded like to me, Jack. He snickered when he said it, like there was something more to it than just a remote. Is it a game or something," she said as she stared at it in his hand. "It's awfully big to be just a remote." She started to get up, and was already reaching out towards it, as if to trade him the note for the remote, which she obviously wanted to inspect.

Jack reacted on instinct in the next moment. He deftly reached over with his right hand and pressed the pause button while his left thumb hit "Alt." Ellen halted mid-motion. She was halfway off the couch, leaning forward. She looked off balance, and Jack was afraid she would fall over. But she was utterly motionless, and caught in the middle of a blink.

Sweat was pouring off Jack's lip. He daubed it, and did some fast thinking. Ellen was going to carry this on until she found out what the remote did. What would he do? He stared at her as he tried to think of a plausible answer to her investigative probe. Then it hit him. Just use the remote!

Jack sat a few minutes, thinking through what he would have to do, and estimating the timing. Then he gingerly hefted the remote, turned off the television, then positioned his fingers, and pressed two other keys. Ellen began to move in reverse, pulling the note back towards herself. In normal speed, she backed down into the sofa and reached for the table, where her magazine flew as if magnetized into her hands. She held it in her lap, and began speaking in muted, Asian-sounding tones to Jack, with a question on her face. Still fascinated by the effect, Jack watched her as she neared the beginning of their conversation, and then sat back with the magazine, biting her fingernail as she read, which she did when no one was watching. Jack would have been in the bathroom at this point. Momentarily, Ellen's face adopted a quizzical look as she stared over toward Jack's chair.

Then she turned toward the end table, reached over to it, and appeared to be retrieving the cordless phone. She pressed one of the buttons, which before had disconnected the call, and put the phone to her face, and began talking to Larry, while scribbling, or un-scribbling on the scratch paper. Jack leaned up to watch, as her hands moved and the ink literally came off the paper and disappeared into the point of the pen. She spoke into the phone several times, then looked at it, pressed the on-off button, and placed it on the table. Then she turned back away from the table, and was immediately absorbed in the magazine.

Now! Jack thought. He pressed Alt-pause. Ellen stopped what little motion she had invested in reading and fingering the pages. Jack got up, went behind her, and picked up the phone. Later, she would not see the phone disappear, since her back was to it. He only hoped she had not taken any special notice of its being on the table earlier. Leaving Ellen paused, Jack carried the phone back into the hall and into the bathroom, putting it on the counter. Now, *he* could answer the call instead of Ellen. He returned to the den, just within sight of her, but at the corner of the hall, and pressed Alt-play. Ellen slowly began moving again, as Jack ducked out of sight. Then he tiptoed down the hall and re-entered the bathroom. Closing the door, he stood waiting for the phone to ring.

When three minutes or more had passed and the phone had not rung, Jack began trying to figure out what had happened. He was certain he had not "rewound" Ellen's movements to more than fifteen seconds before the phone had rung. What was the hold up?

Then it occurred to him what was taking place. He had established the fact that the remote froze only action in the immediate vicinity and even then stopped only physical motion. But Larry of Larry's Lectronics Lair was not in the room but at his store. Ellen may have backed up, but Larry's life and movement went on normally. There would be no repeat phone call because Larry's call took place only once.

As to what had happened to the call, Jack wasn't certain. Ellen *had* answered the call, without question. That, Jack supposed, could not change. But what was to be made of the fact that Ellen was now reliving that time, but not talking on the phone, as she had before? It seemed a contradiction, but Jack assumed she—and he, obviously—were in another "time line." This was what it would have been like, and *was* like, had the phone not been the den. Except, of course, that in this time line, the phone does not ring, because Jack had manipulated time and motion in a very local way. He refused to think about the implications that there was some other *Ellen* in another time line, answering the phone, pressing another *Jack* for an answer—he wondered how his alter ego would get out of it!

Waiting another minute or so to make certain that the phone was not, in fact, going to ring, finally Jack left it on the counter, and returned to the den. Ellen was still reading. The kids could be heard downstairs fighting over the details of their make-believe game. Jack sat down, and picked up the remote. He switched on the TV.

Ellen glanced up and took a gander at the oversized gadget. "It's so large. What in the world does it need to be that big for?"

"Extra range, I guess," said Jack. And because it is a prototype, it's probably not designed as compactly as the final model will be." He hoped that would settle it.

Jack began to be absorbed in some documentary on the television. As the images of a black-and-white war paraded across the screen, he sorted out what he had just done, and tried to figure out the implications for space and time, to say nothing of his own life. He thought of how handy the remote would be in dealing with arguments. He could pause and plan his answers with more time, or reverse and get out the room before a quarrel started. He could fast-forward through Ellen's tirades, or boring accounts of her day. He could even play with all their minds by fast-forwarding through their news or tales, then rewinding and "guessing" the punch lines. The possibilities were endless.

Lurking around in the back corner of his mind was the realization that such shenanigans would be callous manipulations of his family for entirely selfish reasons. Jack felt moderately guilty about that, and it nagged him around the edges of his consciousness, but he would worry about that later. As long as it didn't really hurt anybody, he had every intention of using technology to improve the quality of his life.

One thing did bother him, however, and that was the lingering question of what was taking place, if anything, in that other "time line," if that's what it was, in which Larry had called him. It was possible, of course, that Jack had simply erased the time from just before Larry's call until Ellen got up to reach for the remote, and erased it selectively in this one little area, replacing it with another, altered segment of time. That explanation seemed to have the least holes in it, but still bothered him. And what was it that Larry wanted to tell him? He could call Larry, of course, and would probably do so tomorrow; but if Larry's call was in another time line, the Larry in *this* time line wouldn't know what Jack was talking about.

Whether in this time line or another, however, Larry *had* called about the remote. What for? Perhaps he simply wanted to warn him about the undocumented features. Maybe the factory had only now discovered them, and Larry was trying to pass along information that Jack was already fully aware of. That sounded reasonable; but Jack had concluded earlier that there couldn't have been any way the manufacturer, and thus Larry, could *not* have known about the motion and time altering powers of the remote. So what was Larry urgent to tell him?

Jack decided it would wait until morning. It was a bit early to go to bed, but after a long, relaxing shower and a raid on the ice box it would feel good to turn in early. The documentary was uninspiring.

It was habit that kicked in next. For a couch potato, the routine of closing up the television shop and turning in for the night came to be automatic routine. The glasses were folded and placed on the chair-side cabinet. The TV guide was tossed to the table top. The foot rest handle was disengaged and the mechanism lowered the rest to the floor. The weary body, accompanied by minor groans and a perfunctory yawn, hoisted itself to the front edge of the chair, and just before rising, the fingers found the "off" button and the screen went dark.

All this he did, almost without thinking, while Ellen, poring over her own reading, paid no attention. But this evening, because of the repeated exercise of new motions, there was a slight amendment of the routine. For when Jack's practiced fingers went to command the television to turn off, he absent-mindedly combined the depression of the "off" button with the newer Alt button as well.

The question of what Larry of Larry's Lectronics Lair had called to tell Jack was now answered, for the record at least. The matter of Jack's manipulation of his family for selfish reasons was resolved, perhaps not by a method that all parties would have found acceptable, but resolved nevertheless. And the potential danger of the remote, by misuse or accident, was both realized and eliminated, in a single event.

For in a micro-second from the depression of that last sequence of buttons on the amazing prototype remote control, molecules of corporeal substance suddenly flew away from each other as if repelled by some fundamental polarity. Substance dissipated into the air, and the instrument of danger and source of manipulation slipped out into the transparency of non-existence. For among all the potent, undocumented features of the remote, its one ungrounded feature now took effect. Jack Logan's remote, along with Jack Logan himself, simply disappeared.

# The Switch

When the door slammed, Ford Redfern stared at it as if he could see his wife, Becky, stalk off beyond it, back to her bedroom where she would no doubt gather up laundry. She did laundry whenever she and Ford fought. It was as if she believed washing clothes would cleanse her soul, as well; or perhaps she thought she would "wash that man right out of my hair," or life, perhaps. For his part, Ford tended more toward brooding, cursing at his dog, standing in the driveway and launching a single, vivid epithet directly toward the heavens, awakening neighbors if appropriately timed, and always attracting the ire of the mutt next door, which barked and howled in either irritation or sympathy, he couldn't say which. After he got it off his chest, he calmed down within an hour. But until then, neither he nor Becky would speak. Then, as if nothing had happened, one would ask the other where the TV Guide was, an answer would follow, and life would continue normally.

Tonight's argument and subsequent pitched battle were over his mother, specifically the attention he paid to her at the expense of his wife. Another week, and the same shoe on the other foot would be the topic, or the amount of gas in the car, or the amount of money in the bank, or their recalcitrant daughter, or their wayward son, or their failure to do anything interesting, or an accusation that one of them enjoyed *too much* that was interesting, or a mess one of them had made, or one of hundreds of things strung end to end and repeated endlessly, month after month of their eighteen-year marriage. Becky was turning out to be a heartless, critical, domineering, manipulative shrew; and Ford was developing into a violent, petty, shallow, vulgar, tasteless bore, all the things he had seen in his father, John Redfern, and had hoped never to be.

Out in the driveway, he picked his epithet of the evening, and into the eleven o'clock night air, he summoned his pulmonary powers and let go a shriek of disgust, one choice syllable in length. Satisfied, he walked out onto the front lawn, and stood stewing in his frustration. Why were things so bad? Why was Becky so brassy and temperamental? Had she always been that way, and he just didn't see it? Was he so in love with her when he was eighteen and she seventeen that he ignored her latent penchant for nagging and bickering, and married her anyway? He didn't remember their brawling this way the first few years.

But then, he hadn't been so boring and irritable, either. He even bored himself, sometimes, and when he became irritated with Becky, which was sometimes over nothing at all, he felt awful for doing it, but he was reacting not so much to what Becky had done as to what Becky was, what she had become.

Did he love her, he asked the stars, as he looked up into the clear, fall night sky? He couldn't bring himself to say he didn't; but what he felt these days was not much like love. Underneath the accumulated emotions of years of growing bitterness and disappointment, there was probably genuine love; but at present, what he felt was, fearfully, more like familiar contempt.

Many times after fights, Ford came outside, sat in the deep shadow of the towering oak shading half the yard, and imagined himself in another life, another place, another time. On the dark side of the tree from the prying front windows of the house, he sat and rested his head on his knitted hands.

He tried to trace the time line that might have been, if he had made different decisions when he was young. There were other girls, other careers, other places he could have gone. His parents had wanted him to go to college. They had not been entirely enthusiastic about Becky, preferring the daughter of a friend in their church. They had discouraged Ford's plan to get a job with the local machine parts factory and make steady money so he could marry and buy a new truck and leave books and school far behind.

What if he had never had his children, now both in high school, and had married Sharon Crowe, the cheerleader he dated several times, or Lara Talbert, the quiet and studious girl who for some reason seemed to think Ford was fascinating. One of them probably would have been more compatible with Ford, more understanding of him, and less likely to change into the wicked witch in less than a decade after tying the knot. If he had just dated someone else a time or two more, or thought more clearly about his career choices, or perhaps listened to his parents. Maybe he would have been living a different life right now, somewhere in a different time line. If only . . .

Ford decided to walk around the block. He went to the right, down to the corner, and turned left, on the uninhabited street leading to the small neighborhood near the factory, the neighborhood where he had grown up. The road went down, through pitch darkness, to a bottom where there was a bright, sodium-vapor street light, and up again through dwindling light and then deep gloom, finally rising to another circle of light, as the street dead-ended into another, where there were houses. Ford headed down the incline, listening to the cicadas, tree frogs and crickets. Their lonesome chirping belonged to solemn, sleepless nights since time began, and listening to them, Ford was transported in his mind to the high bed of his grandmother's house in Benton, a pine-tree laden community twenty miles from the beach. There in the second-story bedroom that smelled of cedar and old books, he had spent many a night, attempting for an hour or more to drift off, prevented by the humidity and heat, and the worrisome volume of these nighttime creatures outside the window, who had the temerity to sleep in the day and then keep people up all night.

Right now, Ford wished he were back there, ten years old, sleeping in granny's house, knowing that in the morning she would make breakfast, and he and the children who lived behind her house would play, all day, without a care, until they were exhausted, and that when he needed to eat again, his needs would be provided. He would never see the bills for the house, the food, the car, the clothes, and all the rest, if he even realized that these things had to be paid for. His only need of money had been the few cents he spent on bubble gum or an ice cream cone. If he broke something, somebody would fix it. If he lost something, it usually would be replaced. Why wasn't there anyone to do that now? In fact, it had been worse for two years, since his daddy had died, and his mother had been leaning on him for what seemed like everything. Ford had planned on his father being around longer, in spite of the fact that they frequently didn't get along; but now, all of a sudden, Ford was the "daddy," and what vestiges of his childhood he had managed to cling to had been swept away like a dune in a hurricane.

Nearing the bottom of the hill, the light smeared the

darkness away into the underbrush, and the bugs seemed intimidated and less boisterous. But as he left the luminescent oasis behind and started up the hill toward the factory neighborhood, the rhythmic humming and chirping rose to a new height, hypnotic and insistent.

Then, for no particular reason he could figure, the droning, invisible insects faded into the background, and the night air became still, and thin.

In another ten paces, Ford was just at the top of the hill, entering the arc of light from the street lamp on the other side of the intersecting road. He was surprised to see fog up here. Minutes before he peered at the stars above his house, but here there was a bank of fog, like a border around the neighborhood, beginning where the circle of light defined the intersection. Ford became aware that he really couldn't make out the details of houses on the opposite side of the road, and there weren't any houses on the near side, only woods.

He stood at the edge of the circle of light, listening to the sudden silence, and straining to make out the detail of anything inside the foggy block of houses, trees, and parked cars that lay in front of him. He had walked this way many times before, especially when retreating from arguments at home. Never had this neighborhood looked as it did. Something wasn't right.

Ford looked back, thinking perhaps while he was reminiscing about his childhood he had walked down another street, gone a block over, or more, without realizing it. But no, he was where he thought he was. It was, after all, his old haunts; it just didn't look quite as it should.

Then the differences began to dawn on him gradually. It was the street light that gave it away first. All the lights in the little factory community, including the one at the bottom of the hill below his house, were either mercury vapor or sodium vapor lights, the kind that could be kicked by wandering teens and knocked out until they could warm up again. But the light at the center of this glowing cone of foggy luminescence was warm, tungsten gold. There hadn't been a light like that in the entire town for twenty years. What was it doing there?

There was a local historical preservation society, he remembered. Perhaps it had installed a nostalgic street lamp in some of the neighborhoods, but he hadn't heard of such a plan. That didn't prove anything, since he didn't really keep up with community activities, least of all what the culture-crowd was doing.

Yet there it was, a tungsten light, complete with its ribbed pole and decorative base, and all painted deep green. The globe was shaped like a Grecian urn, and had a pebbly surface.

The house closest to the cone of light was high up on the hill, the front door probably more than twenty feet above the sidewalk, though not more than that same distance straight out from the street. Ford had always thought the house interesting, situated as it was. But the house was different, like the light. Built in the thirties, the house had a porch extending the length of its front face, made with tongue-and-grove boards, and bordered by four pillars, brick halfway up and obelisk-shaped wood the rest of the way. To his recollection, those wooden pillars were faded mint green, and badly peeling as well. But the occupants apparently had painted since he last saw the house. The pillars were now a rich, spring-grass green, and the trim on the rest of the house shown brilliant white, even through the fog that hung in the motionless night air.

The yard of the house on the corner, to his left, for years had been the repository, by the owner, of unused, deteriorating cars and car parts, accompanied by plastic tricycles and other toys left daily by the children who lived there. But at the moment, there were no cars to be seen. The yard had been seeded, the tires removed, and the single child's toy visible, tucked up close to the side of the front steps, appeared to be a metal pedal-car.

All this seemed extremely curious. He had apparently missed a major community cleanup effort, and obviously had not participated in it, as a cursory inspection of his own yard and house would show instantly.

Something moved slightly in the shadow of the steps leading up from the sidewalk across the street to the house high on the hill. Sitting on the first step was a small dog, peering across to where Ford stood, just outside the rim of light and just below the intersection. The dog's attention was riveted on Ford's position, but he was cocking his head from side to side, pricking his ears, and remained silent, as if trying to determine just what, if anything, Ford was.

Ford stepped back, farther from the ring of light. The dog suddenly stood on all fours, looked into the darkness, then side to side, as if whatever he had been looking at had disappeared. Ford thought to himself that a dog's night vision was good, and that surely he had not been completely obscured in the dark. He stepped back to where he had stood before. The dog suddenly turned toward him, jumped in place as dogs do when about to run away, and then stood stock still. Ford took another step toward the intersection, and into the light. As he did, the little dog jumped in pure fright, and with only a light squeal rather than a bark, he disappeared up the hill and under the front porch of the house.

Something terribly strange was taking place. Ford seemed drawn into the light and onto this street so strangely refurbished. He took three or four steps forward, and as he did, a shiver coursed through him from head to toe, actually beginning with his leading toe and continuing over the rest of his body as he came into the light. He suddenly felt awash in light, as if illuminated on the inside as well, yet with a cool, invigorating tingle. The sensation lasted a moment, and then left him.

Standing beneath the street lamp now, he looked again at the houses on the street. There was no trace of the fog that had been obscuring them partially, and every detail of them was sharp, in the contrast of the light put off by the lamp, and by the moon overhead. Ford had never seen fog lift, or rather, dissipate, so rapidly, and whipped around to see if it had simply moved down into the low bottom of the street he had come up. Indeed, he could see down to the other street lamp, the sodium-vapor one, but the details were fuzzy. Ford realized he was looking *through* the fog as much as into it, and was surprised he had not realized before that it was just a billow of condensation rising perhaps from a nearby sewer grate, or coming out of the glade nearby. Dismissing it for the moment, he turned back to the neighborhood.

What before had seemed so strange to him, since it differed from his recent memory, he began to realize now was deceptively familiar, only now from his more distant memory. This was what his neighborhood had looked like twenty-five or thirty years ago.

Ford was quickly becoming irrational. He suddenly didn't question the reason for all the fresh paint and repairs, the yard cleanups and utility replacements. In fact, he began to realize, quite against anything sensible at all, that none of this was new at all, but really quite old. Whether by some quirk of time and space, or magic, and it didn't matter which, Ford Redfern was staring at the edge of his childhood neighborhood, as it was three decades or so ago.

One block over was his boyhood house. His mother, Hazel, had inherited it from her parents just about the time she and his dad had married, and they moved into it after their honeymoon. It had been razed after being destroyed partially in a fire the year Ford graduated from high school. His parents had built on the same spot, a dull, brick cubicle with no character at all, but air conditioned and wall-to-wall carpeted. It hadn't been home since. Remembering the old house, Ford broke into a sprint, sailing around the corner and up the hill. He felt abruptly youthful, and refused to debate with his own mind the absurdity of the notion that he actually could be in his childhood neighborhood, and in the time of his childhood at that. If there were any reality at all to what was happening, he would take it all in while it was accessible.

As he passed the alley between blocks, the phenomenon continued, consistent. The alley of his present day was paved with asphalt; but this one was large gravel, with a grassy strip down the middle between the tire trails.

Puffing slightly, he came to his street, Vernon St., and looked up at the sign. It was the old green metal, with a framed letter area at the top, just as he remembered from years ago. Ford slowed to a walk, but kept up a quick pace, nervously heading down the block where he had lived, or did live. His house was five down on the left. As he passed the first house, the Tyler's, he believed, then the second, the Green's, where "Stingray" Green had lived, his legs began to shake. He couldn't help it. Something in his body knew this was an extraordinary moment, and both feared and anticipated it.

The third house was "Smiley" Martin's, a boy he biked and swum with, who had gone to live in Kentucky when Ford was in the tenth grade. There it was, complete with the vines that covered the west wall completely, and which could be climbed in and out of Smiley's bedroom window.

The fourth house, next to his, belonged to Mr. Barnes, an old man whose main concern in life was to keep Ford and Smiley out of his yard. Barnes had died fifteen years ago, and his house turned into a duplex and inhabited by a string of biker-gang types and other malcontents. But there was Mr. Barnes' deep blue Dodge, sitting in the fine-gravel driveway, ready for him to drive it out in the morning as he always did.

Ford stopped. Next to Mr. Barnes' house was his own. In the diminished light from the corner lamppost the little frame house sat small and humble, the screen of its porch suffering from rust discoloration and its slate roof faintly reflecting in grayish tones the light from the moon. Ford realized suddenly that unlike any of the houses on the street so far, there was light in his, a single lamp in the front room, which served as living room, den, and sometimes bedroom when family guests came and he had to vacate his bed.

Any fears of some sort of complication arising from his seeing his past were dissolved in the pressing need, indeed the urgent emotional drive he had to see who was inside the front room. Crossing the grassy yard, he crept lower and lower as he neared the window. Through the gauzy sheers his mother had always hung in the front windows of the house, he could see the lamp on the table beside their sofa. Neither looked exactly as he remembered, but perhaps his memories, like most people's, had been edited by time. On the end of the sofa, her young features hazily apparent through the curtains, sat his mother, Hazel, cutting coupons out of a newspaper flyer. On the other end of the sofa was a darker shape, harder to see but presumably his dad. He was propped up in the corner with a pillow, holding a small Coca-Cola bottle in his hand, and watching the television that was nearer the front wall, facing away from Ford. The images from the set made flickering effects on his parents' faces and the furniture in the room.

Ford was mesmerized looking at the two, obviously long before his father's death, and long enough ago that he assumed he himself must have been no more than seven or eight. Maybe younger.

Ford looked around the room. There was no one else in it that he could see. If the neighborhood were dark because of the late hour, "he" must be in bed. While he was pondering the absurd wonderment of this whole scene, a small figure emerged from the darkened opening of the stairwell. The child was clad in what appeared to be a long nightgown, and had long, silky hair. She may have been six or seven. She bounced down the two bottom stairs, and bounded over to the sofa, climbing onto the reclining figure of the man. He opened his arms and welcomed her with a bear hug, and the first sounds Ford heard from within the room were the girl's happy words, "Goo'night, daddy," after which she disengaged from his embrace and jumped across the sofa to receive a similar, more delicate version from Ford's mother.

*Daddy?* Who was this girl? Ford had no sister! He didn't have a brother, either. His mother had experienced a difficult pregnancy and had required surgery afterward that left her unable to have more children. That *was* his mother, wasn't it?

He looked at the woman more closely. Situated under the lamp, her features were plain enough, even though gauzy. That was his mother, thirty years younger, to be sure, but his mother, no doubt. And the man on the darker end of the sofa? Surely . . .

Suddenly he began to hear them begin a conversation. If it had not been so graveyard quiet he could not have heard them, but every word was audible.

"Oh, honey, she's so precious," his mother said, turning to her husband.

"She takes after her mother," he said.

"No, I mean it," his mother insisted.

"So do I."

"Besides," she continued, "you had *something* to do with it, after all."

The exchange didn't sound like anything his parents said to each other, especially when he had ever been around. But then, the man on the other end of the sofa didn't exactly sound like the father he had known.

"Honey," Hazel went on, "do you think Angela will miss having a brother or sister?"

"There are lots of children who don't have brothers or sisters," he said.

"I know, but I just hope she doesn't think we cheated her. I feel bad that I—"

"Hazel," he said, "don't blame yourself. It wasn't your fault. Some people aren't meant to have but one child. She's that much more special. And she'll be just fine."

Hazel sniffed and held back tears. "Oh, I hope so," she said. The "daddy" on the other end of the sofa got up and came toward her chair.

"Come here, baby," he said to her, and she got up and met

him and they embraced. He looked at her up close, and said, "She'll do great. She's got you. And you've got me!" He chuckled. And he sounded nothing like Ford's dad.

Ford squinted and pored over the features of the man inside his living room. It suddenly dawned on him that this man, obviously married to his young mother, was not his father. And the little girl, obviously their daughter, was no one he knew of.

They were talking again. "And to think," said the man who was not his father, "that you might have married John Redfern."

"Michael Parker, you hush!" she teased. And they kissed lightly, and went back to their warm spots on either end of the overstuffed sofa.

Ford was stunned. This was not his father, John Redfern. The girl, Angela, was not his sister. The house was his—at least, it was his mother's, but there were odd differences in furnishing. Everything since he came through the mist or fog, or whatever it was on the corner one block over, had been authentically his past. But this was clearly not right.

Without actually thinking about it, Ford was backing away from the window. Then he turned and ran back toward the corner of the yard, past Mr. Barnes' house, faster past Smiley Martin's and Stingray Green's, and rounded the block, dashing downhill at breakneck speed, cutting across the corner lot, bounding over the front wall of its lawn, and punching into the ring of light under the green lamppost that was out of place in time. Heaving and gasping volumes of the fresh night air, he realized the fear and anxiety that had come over him. It was an undefined, but profound respect for his personal history. He was conscious of a certain dread of what might have been, not if *he* had made different decisions in his life, but if *other* people—like his own mother!—had done so. Suddenly, his life didn't seem so bad. Heck, his wife didn't seem so bad. And his children were great!

Peering nervously across the street to the hill he had ascended into this nightmarish place of his past, or *somebody's* past, he saw, much to his relief, that the vague cloud of fog was still situated just below the intersection. Through it, he could see the next street light at the bottom of the hill, in soft focus because of the mist, but reassuringly a sodium-vapor light, belonging to the neighborhood of his adult life. Beyond it, no doubt, his house and family lay, just as he had left them.

Not willing to bet on how long this anomaly in time would remain, however, and having had enough of this distorted representation of the past, Ford began running again, at full steam, toward the misty cloud. He pierced it with a long stride, and again felt that tingling, light sensation that had washed over him when he had unwittingly traversed it before. No sooner had it swept through his limbs than it was gone, but Ford didn't stop to consider it, or to look back to see if the neighborhood at the edge of his childhood haunts had changed back to the present. He continued, instead, to race down the hill, back up the hill, and around the corner to his house, his muscles straining and tightening as he went up the driveway toward his home.

Mercifully for his no-longer-twenty-something body, he stopped halfway up and looked up at the silhouette of his house in the dark shadows of the trees, cast by a three-quarter moon. It looked better. It even looked more well kept, so relieved was he to be back.

Inside, no doubt Becky had left the wash running and headed toward bed. In the morning she would have gotten over their row earlier. In his great relief to be back, Ford felt a rush of joy so intense that he was certain he would approach his marriage with a new love, his children with a new affection, and his life with new maturity. He had the impulse to rush in, embrace them all, no doubt to their total bewilderment, and tell them he loved them. But with a pulse rate of about 130 and sweat beaded up on his head, he would have to explain why he had been running, and he wasn't certain he could, or ever would, relate what had just happened to him.

He treaded quietly over to the big oak, and sat down in his familiar place to let his cardiovascular system return to normal. Head in hands, the images of his experience moments ago swirled in his brain.

After a moment, calmed more quickly than he would have thought, he got up and walked back up the driveway around to the back of the house, and he slipped in the back door in the darkness.

Everyone had gone to bed and the lights were all out. He found his way through the kitchen and into the den, bumping into a piece of furniture somebody had discourteously left out of place. Trying to avoid the squeaky board in the hallway he surprised himself by succeeding for once. Feeling for his bedroom door, he pushed it open, and in the blackness within, he reached out and waved his hand slowly until it touched the bedpost. Then he stood in that spot, pulled his tennis shoes off, leaving his socks on, slipped out of his jeans, which felt unusually tight, and leaving the rest of his clothes on, moved around to his side of the bed, found the edge of the covers, lifted them quietly, and slipped in, trying not to wake his spouse.

Once he was still, however, his mate stirred and turned

toward him. A hand touched his arm, and gently rubbed him. Evidently, he had been forgiven.

Then his sleepy spouse said, "I had begun to think you weren't coming to bed at all." And the voice was the distinctly resonant, bass pitch of a man.

Involuntarily, Ford shuddered, and his mind went numb, as a pain of shock coursed through his chest. The man next to him, where Becky should have been, said, "You're shaking, honey, what is it?"

And Ford, who wanted to scream, 'Who are you and what have you done with my wife,' raised his hand to clutch his throbbing chest, and his voice stopped short in his throat. For his chest was now amply endowed with feminine charms. And over the smooth, hairless skin of his delicate neck were long tresses of silken hair.

And the man next to him in the bed, with a last, roving caress of *his?* body, and giving away nothing but that he was totally familiar with the curves and softness he found there, said, "G'night Angela; I love you," and then rolled over and went to sleep.

*The Switch*

# The Valentine

Chilling winds of late January swept up through the tightly grouped buildings of Glenn State College, carrying with them the last leaves never raked from the fall, scattered crystals of snow from the rooftops like shrapnel from an icy bomb, and the coat tails of Dr. Palmer Wagner, professor of philosophy. The gusts hurried his steps involuntarily, helping him down the stairway from the main courtyard, into the parking lot where his Volvo awaited, not quite warm but shielded from the chilling train of wind, rushing through the campus terrain.

His cheeks beginning to be numb from the assault of moisture and cold, Palmer broke into a trot, taking his hands out of his coat pockets just in case he slipped and needed them to break his fall. The jogging made his loose clothes flop in great jerking movements, and everything in his pants pockets shook. The considerable mass of change in his right pocket began to jingle and ring as if he were a prospector showing off his new bag of gold. Instinctively his hands went down in cups to hold the change in his right pocket and the keys in his left to the fronts of his legs, as he continued the short-stroked sprint toward his car.

His mind raced off in another direction. It was so many years ago. He couldn't have been more than six years old. He knew that because he was in first grade at the time. He was behind a tree in a front yard. His father, Murray Wagner, was beside him. He was urging Palmer to run to the door.

"Just run up there, son, and put it in the door, then ring the doorbell. Then run back here." The elder Mr. Wagner whispered the words conspiratorially in the crisp night air, as the two of them crouched in the darkness at the base of the pine tree. In front of them was a large, Williamsburg-style house, a few rooms warmly lit at this mid-evening hour. In Palmer's hand was an envelope. Earlier that evening, he had sat at his family's kitchen table, preparing the envelope and its special contents for this very hour, scrawling the words on the card inside, after asking the spelling of each one, all three of them. The card was the seasonal red and white in color; the words, apart from his name, were these: "I love you."

This was a significant confession for a six-year-old boy in the first grade; but there was no one quite like Emily Carter, and it was Valentine's Day night, which emboldened secret lovers everywhere. All the students had brought valentines to school that day, but it was custom to take that one special valentine to the home of the beloved and deliver it in person. Well, sort of in person. Actually, the procedure was a bit more surreptitious. A boy—girls didn't ordinarily perform the ritual—took the valentine by night to the home of the object of his affection, crept up to her porch, rang the doorbell, left the card in the screen door, and dashed to the safety of surrounding darkness, or, if proximity made it possible, ran home lickety split.

Thus it was that Palmer was there, on that Valentine's Day night many years ago, hiding behind a pine tree, ready to deliver his missive of love. His parents knew he was sweet on Emily, and finding it a sweet gesture, they had helped him create his card, and then Mr. Wagner had agreed to drive him across the boulevard to the next neighborhood to Emily Carter's house, where they now stood. Only now, Palmer was scared to go to the door.

Mr. Wagner prompted him several times, prodded him, encouraged him, but Palmer's knees were shaking, partly from the cold but mostly from nervous fear. "You take it, dad!" he had told him, "I don't want to. You take it!"

Murray Wagner sighed with frustration, and perhaps some understanding, and said, "Give me the card." It was then that he darted from underneath the pine tree, a big man jogging with short steps through the dew-laden grass toward a darkened front porch, with his hands cupped over the fronts of his pants pockets, trying to damper the sound of keys and change. Palmer saw his dark form on the porch, placing the envelope securely in the screen door, pushing the lighted bell, and then quickly hopping down the steps and sprinting back to the shadowy base of the tree, all the way his change jingling in the muffled confines of his pants pockets.

There was rarely, if ever, a time when his change jingled in his own pockets that Palmer did not envision that night long ago, in the front yard of his first boyhood girlfriend's house, sending his message of love by proxy. But few times since then had his sentiment of love been as pure, as filled with the raw fear of self-disclosure, or as laden with the passion of the soul. Even after he was old enough to know what true love should be like, he knew he had found it spiked with base passion and desire, watered down with artificial sentiments, or disguising acts of conformity. He had loved for the convenience of making love; he had imagined love rather than be lonely when everyone else was in love; or he had called some good friendship love because his parents or everyone else expected him to settle down, both to tame the potential playboy and to assure society that he was not something other than heterosexual.

Finally, Palmer had, indeed, settled down. After dating around, he married while still in graduate school, moving into an apartment near the Glenn State campus. His wife opened her own art store in a quaint section of town, naming it "Daisy's," for no good reason except that she liked daisies. It earned her the nickname, "Daisy," and even Palmer called her by it.

The first few years of their marriage were dominated by the busy schedule of Palmer's doctoral studies, his wife's struggle to build her business from scratch, and the eventual, only partly intended arrival of their first child, Daniel, who took up time and energy they had not thought they had. In fact, they both believed they were engaging in deficit spending over their time budget, and that eventually the debt would have to be paid.

It was paid, not through the arrival of some crisis of marital vows, but in the slow onslaught of apathy, purchased with unintentional but regular payments of inattention. He had eased into a life of fluctuating interest and boredom, like the flowing and ebbing of tides, which had cast upon the undistinguished beach of his years the detritus of hardly memorable events, which were themselves becoming covered over with the proverbial sands of time, only the remnants of their reality protruding above the surface of his memory. It was difficult sometimes for him to grasp those memories and believe that he had been that person, done those things, had those experiences, possessed those feelings. They seemed like another world, and another person who lived in it. Palmer wondered if anyone else ever felt this way.

The frozen latch of his car door gave way under the second tug. Palmer slid into the windless cold of the Volvo, which was somehow the symbol both of his successful career and of his confinement to the mundane. As he sat there, staring out the rapidly fogging windshield, he wondered if the days of his youth were completely unrecoverable, if the warmth and simple excitement of something like childhood romance or youthful adventure were beyond anything but hazy remembrance.

Palmer's experience of monotony encompassed his entire life, now, but it seemed most significant in his marriage. There was no trouble—at least none worth speaking of. There simply was nothing remarkable. And now that Daniel had been out on his own for a year, it was just the two of them again, and the un-remarkableness of their lives seemed all the more pronounced.

Every once in a while his wife hinted at her own realization of it. And while she had her own form of imprisonment in normalcy, she was unable to think of herself as having contributed to it, feeling that, like romantic overtures, the responsibility for injecting excitement into a marriage was principally on a man's shoulders. She never got angry over it, just a bit depressed in her nostalgia.

She would say, "We never do anything. We never go anywhere." In fact, Daisy had turned down the prospect of several trips, owing to her inability to get away from her art store or from her own personality, which was infused with some fear of change or of the unknown.

Palmer frequently spent Saturdays in his office, where he had complete quiet to read, both books for himself and papers of students. His absence didn't encourage his relationship with Daisy. She tried to overcome her disappointment with a show of enthusiasm: she had been the one who came up with ideas about the little jaunts they took or day activities that occupied them very few Saturdays out of the year. But she herself had fallen into a rhythm of unbroken habits, an uninspired pattern of life that compounded Palmer's own, and made of their lives together something flat and wearisome.

It dulled the sharp sense of passion they once had, when they still felt excitement at each other's mere touch. Once they had felt almost indistinguishable from the couples who walked hand in hand, or considerably closer, or stood in the darkened corners of campus walls and buildings on warm summer nights and cold winter ones alike. Not only were they young enough then to pass for students, but they were sufficiently filled with the gleaming-eyed ardor of young love that they glowed with the same fire and put off the same heat.

Now, they felt the way they, when they were teens, thought their parents looked—like quintessential adults, lacking what could be realistically called sexuality, settled into a spiraling routine of necessity and drudgery that would only end in death.

The Volvo was not becoming any warmer while Palmer stared at the campus lights that had now become great, luminescent blobs on the surface of the foggy, frosty glass. He turned the key and the engine began to hum dependably, the heater shortly delivering relief to his chilled shins.

On the way home, which was now in a suitably collegiate subdivision where half the faculty lived, he went along Circumference Drive, where his old apartment was. There were dozens of them, in units side by side and back to back, mirror images and double reverses of one another. As he came alongside the first of them, about half were lit by porch lights, half not, as couples had barricaded themselves against winter behind their doors by this hour. When he spotted his old unit, there was a couple at the threshold, he with his keys trying to find the keyhole by the light of the moon, and she, bundled up in a long coat, hugging him from behind, not making his job easier with the jostling, but not able to keep from embracing him as they prepared to enter their little world, the workshop of their togetherness, the playground of their love, the Eden of their companionship. It occurred to Palmer that the ferocious and yet tender passions of these young, married students made them every one unique, whirling pairs of emotional energy and bright, colorful examples of the beauty of life, in stark contrast to the dead, dull, carbon-copy units in which they lived. The apartments were somehow not able to contain or tame them, and the only life the drab Monopoly-like houses had was the palpable vibrance of the couples in love inside them.

Palmer saw them as he remembered himself and his wife. And it struck him suddenly that he had not driven this way by mistake, had not jogged noisily to his car by accident, had not sat in reverie, reliving ancient memories of a first grade romance with Emily Carter, had not waxed emotional over the passions of his college days, or over the burning ardor of his early married years, for no reason other than the propensity of human beings to nostalgia. He had not come by this intense longing to regain the unpredictable, impetuous love of his wife and their adventure into the daily unknown, for no purpose.

Perhaps in spite of his academic commitment to philosophy, he believed in a guiding force beyond the control of man, in a god, or in God, if you will. He believed because he had seen before the evidence of some unseen hand benevolently manipulating events, creating repeating intersections of thought and happenstance, in a preponderance of evidence that led him to conclusions and decisions. Just now, he could sense that hand. It had moved him through a series of catalysts to his thought, capping off weeks of deepening melancholy. It had prodded him to think longingly of the way things once had been, and to desire more than ever to recapture a feeling and excitement he had thought gone for good. And this unseen hand had brought out from his mind an oft-remembered scene, of a valentine, a furtive visit to a childhood sweetheart's house, and the vivid feeling of the anxiousness of simple love.

In a moment of serendipitous revelation, Palmer saw a valentine as the thing to symbolize the recapture of a youthful sense of love. How many years had it been since he and his wife had exchanged so simple a thing as a valentine—or had they ever? It was like the dozens of other things they had discarded or quit doing along the way, perhaps because without saying it they believed them to be silly, childish, unnecessary.

A valentine. He would present her with a valentine, some well-planned, lovingly chosen gift, perhaps not even something that could be fit in a box or slipped into an envelope, but a valentine nonetheless. He would invest it with significance much greater than the valentine itself and let her know that it was a symbol of himself. He would plan it with precision and secrecy, and deliver it with loving delight.

It little mattered that at the moment, Palmer didn't know exactly what the valentine would be. In fact, what it might turn out to be was far less important than what it would mean—what it already meant. For what it would mean, to him and to his wife, was nothing less than the reclamation of love.

In a swirling joy that looked for all the world like hope, he finished the short drive to his comfortable home and slipped in the back door. Daisy had gone to bed, probably shortly past nine, and it was nearly ten. In the dark of his bedroom, Palmer shed his clothes by the bed, slipped between the covers, prompting only slight stirring from the other side of the mattress, and drifted rapidly to sleep, moving from excited thoughts and plans into dreams of the same. And throughout the night, his own heart's revival of love's excitement continued, deep within his very soul.

They barely crossed paths in the morning, Mr. and Mrs. Palmer Wagner. She rose earlier, by habit, than he, and went to her store a couple of hours before it opened, to get a jump on the day and conduct the business that always lay underneath the visible sales and display most people see. He rose later, not having had for several years any early morning classes, the newer professors and associates being stuck with them as part of their dues before attaining tenure.

Palmer ate more than usual, making himself a luxurious breakfast of fruit, cereal, then a small omelet. He liked to cook, and frequently had to do so because of his and his wife's mismatched schedules. While he ate, he scratched on a pad beside him, outlining his valentine plan. It had hatched largely during the night, in vivid dreams that stretched into consciousness as he moved from darkness into the light of morning. Thinking about breakfast, he added another note to his list of things to do. Then he washed up the things he had used, got his coat and scarf, and headed toward the door.

On the way out, he paused to look at the calendar hung by the back entrance. He turned over the page to reveal the new month. It was now the first day of February. He had two weeks to prepare.

The days went by rapidly, but he worked his plan on schedule, spending time on the phone, dropping by locations in town, having several conferences with people in the philosophy department, and dropping in on the art department. If his wife suspected anything special was underway, she didn't say so, although Palmer appeared more cheery at home, made more conversation about her and her work, and even chanced discussing future trips or getaways. Occasionally, she would cast an odd look his direction, and ever so slightly shake her head to herself as if thinking, "No, it couldn't be."

When the evening of February 13 arrived, he was finished with the last details, except for one. Before he left his office, as the last beams of a disappearing sun struck the bookcase on the wall opposite his window, and slid upward until the shadows melted into a dim haze and disappeared, Palmer sat down at his desk, and opened a box of crayons.

It was nearing eight o'clock as Palmer opened the front door and walked into his house. Daisy was working at the computer, putting together copy for an ad to be placed in the local newspaper. She briefly inquired about his day, and he about hers, and they made small talk about trivial matters, mail, an upcoming faculty get-together, whether to have their television repaired or replaced.

Then she turned her swivelling chair away from the monitor, and looked quizzically at Palmer. "You have been...different lately. What is it?"

"What do you mean, different?" he asked. Of course, he knew he had been more upbeat, even though he was hiding the excitement he had about surprising her with his valentine, and he was certain she had noticed he was not quite as sedate, not as edgy or cynical as he had been two weeks before.

"Thoughtful, I think," she said, "perhaps even solicitous." She said it with a curious glance that combined her obvious appreciation with a lurking sense of suspicion. And not being reluctant to speak her mind, she added, with playfulness that thinly disguised a tentative seriousness, "It's almost like you're fooling around."

Palmer wrinkled his brow, affronted by the half-hearted insinuation. "I hardly think I would be paying more attention to you if I had found someone elsewhere to give it to instead."

"On the contrary," she answered, "that's exactly what you would be doing—to deflect suspicion."

Palmer turned his mouth into a wry grin. "Then it's a lose-lose situation, isn't it? If I don't show you attention, I'm in the doghouse. If I do show you attention, I'm in the doghouse. What would I have to do to prove I wasn't hiding something?"

Daisy looked at him over the tops of her half-height reading glasses as if she didn't understand the question. Past her eyes he tried to see some unspoken query. He thought perhaps she was thinking, 'Why in the world would you pay more attention to me unless you *were* hiding something?' But he couldn't be certain.

"I don't know," she said hesitantly, "maybe it's just been so long." Then, becoming self-conscious, she turned back in her chair to her work, and changed the subject. "There's stew on the stove. I kept it warm. And bread in the bun warmer. And you can have the last of the coffee. I can't afford to drink any more of it—I'll be in bed by nine thirty."

And that, essentially, was the end of conversation for the

evening.

Long before dawn, Palmer awoke to the beeping of his watch in his ear. He wore it to bed, and since he always put his left arm under the pillow under his head, he could hear the watch's alarm just enough to wake up, but it wouldn't be heard at all on the other side of the mattress. It was four thirty. He smoothly and quietly slipped out of bed and went down the hall, where he dressed in the guest room, having taken his clothes there before retiring. Closing the doors between the bedroom wing of the house and the living areas, he began the first surprise of the day.

When Daisy awoke at her usual hour, quarter till six, she didn't at first realize Palmer wasn't in the bed. She tiptoed around the room until the light from the bathroom spilled onto the bedside, revealing his absence. She talked to herself.

"Now what do you suppose he got up at this hour for? Unless he went to sleep over one of his books and never made it to bed." Robed and slippered, she padded down the hall, opened the doors to the den, and was met with the distinctive scent of chipped beef. In the kitchen, the stove and counters were spotless, but on the table at her place, still steaming, was a plate with poached eggs on English muffin, topped with chipped beef in cream sauce. It was a favorite of hers from years back, which she never seemed to have time to make for herself, much less for Palmer. It was accompanied by a small serving of hominy, a Southern delicacy she never bought because Palmer couldn't stand it, a garnish of orange slice and parsley, and a small bowl of cooked apples. A cup of coffee sat, freshly poured, by the plate. She stared un-comprehendingly.

The cuisine, plus the fact that Palmer's car was gone, was adequate proof that the breakfast was hers and that he had made it. After the initial shock wore off, she sat down and consumed the meal, thinking to herself all the while that Palmer owed her an explanation.

Then again, she thought while she got dressed for work, maybe she should just take it at face value, and appreciate it. Had she gotten too old to appreciate nice gestures? Or was Palmer bribing her?

At six forty-five she walked through the kitchen toward the back door and the garage. Just as she reached for the door knob, she stopped and took a step backward. Something posted on the side of the refrigerator was different. It was the writing in red ink on the calendar that hung there amidst all sorts of coupons, outdated notes to herself, and new recipes she would never try. There was a circle around the following weekend, where Palmer had written, "Today and every Saturday belongs to us alone."

A wash of curiosity and longing swept through her, as she realized that this was, after all, Valentine's Day. It had been years since Palmer had been this attentive, even on February 14, but it was nice to remember. Daisy realized at this point that she hadn't done anything for him, and both because of the sadness of that and the happiness of being treated to these nice little surprises, she found herself dabbing teary eyes, as she turned the lock on the door and hurried to her car in the brisk air.

At her store she opened the front door to the usual, faint smell of wood and paint, and made her way into her glassed-in cubicle at the back, where she did her morning work. The message light on her phone was blinking, which was not uncommon. She dialed her access codes to play back her messages, while pulling out papers and books to work on. The first piece of voice mail was from a woman:

"Hi, this is Kelly at The Inn at Greenbriar. I'm calling to confirm reservations for the Wagners, a party of two, at the restaurant tonight, at eight o'clock. We'll be looking forward to having you. Bye!"

"Palmer, you sly de- " Daisy started, and then melted into a softer tone, "you sweet guy." A small, involuntary shiver shook her shoulders. She archived the message and then began going over her day planner. Every few minutes she would find herself staring off in distraction, a little smile lurking in the corners of her mouth.

About ten o'clock, as a few customers were moving about, Daisy checked her mail drop in the storefront. Among the invoices and catalogs there was a heavy envelope marked "Personal," from the Longwood Travel Agency. She opened it using her finger like a letter opener, and scanned the letter, expecting it not to be personal at all, but just a bulk mail come-on for some cruise. Instead, it began:

"Dear Mrs. Palmer, We're excited that you and your husband have decided to take a custom trip through New England. We've worked out the fall dates you requested, and booked all the hotels and transportation fares. The luxury train ride on your third day sounds especially romantic, and we're sure you'll love the falls, the blazing Autumn mountains, and the rocky coasts."

First breakfast, then a promise of more time together, then a gourmet meal, and now a romantic trip—the only things he had left out were jewelry and flowers.

The door opened behind her, producing the quaint sound of a jingling, ancient bell, attached at the top of the jamb. It was John, the man from the college art department who occasionally delivered artwork Daisy had bought from students in the ceramics workshop.

"I hope you have my vase," she said.

"Yep, this is it," he said, and put the heavily padded package down at the office door. "Doc Summers says be sure to take out all the packing inside.

Daisy signed for the package, a formality that seemed embarrassing between friends, and John left. She undid the fasteners on the crate, and extracted a tall, slim vase she had seen one of the art students working on two weeks ago. She had offered the girl a handsome sum on the spot. She had wanted to take it home and keep it for herself, but when Palmer said, "Yeah, it would make a nice place to put my umbrella," she decided it would grace the store instead—in fact, her office to be exact.

She reached down in the tall, thin vase to extract crushed paper packing, wondering at the same time, why put packing inside a vase, where there's nothing to shake around? Nothing, perhaps, except the small box she grasped as her hands balled up the last of the paper at the bottom. She extracted the white box, tied up with a red string. Inside was a deep blue jewelry box. And inside the jewelry box, when she finally opened her eyes after opening it, was a dazzling luminescent opal ring, with the most exquisite, lacy filigree setting. She slipped it on with trembling hands. It seemed to burn. At least, she herself was beginning to feel warm.

Now where were the flowers? What a shameful thought. What had she done to deserve all this?

Periodically throughout the afternoon she peered out the front window, looking for a florist's van. When by five it didn't arrive, she smiled, chiding herself for trying to predict Palmer, and remembering that he wasn't much for flowers anyway—never had been.

On the way home she stopped on impulse to buy a small

bottle of "Intimate," a fragrance she used to use and had not bought in years. Though well made up for business, she had not really accommodated the romantic side of clothing and toiletries since... when was it since? Since shortly after Daniel came?

Daisy arrived home by six, and hurried to take a quick bath before Palmer arrived. She had stepped from the steaming tub and wrapped herself in a lush, six-foot towel, when the front doorbell rang.

"Palmer?" she called. If he hadn't come in while she was bathing, she would have to answer the door. Hearing no reply, she grabbed her terry cloth robe, slid into her slippers, and went tentatively to the door. She peeked out.

"Hi. Parker Florist?" the young man said cautiously, noting Daisy was not exactly in clothes suitable to receive visitors. "Delivery for you, Mrs. Wagner." He held out a long, white box.

Daisy took the box, thanked the boy, and shut the door. On the hall table, the box yielded a dozen, long-stemmed red roses, the most delicate and gorgeous she had ever seen. She was aware that, at this point, her valuation of the flowers was less an unbiased judgment than it was an emotional conclusion based on the rest of her day. And Palmer was the best looking man in town, and the greatest husband. Yesterday she wouldn't have volunteered anything out of the ordinary about him. Today, she did, not because of the presents themselves, but because of something they said about him, or something she couldn't quite express. It was like some cargo lost from a boat, suspended deep in a harbor, but now slowly rising to the surface, ready to be rediscovered. There was a warmth to the feeling, an old joy, a vibrancy of youth. She looked at the roses and remembered the single stem Palmer had given her the night he proposed. She had pressed that bud and kept it, though where it was now she wasn't certain. But she had pledged that her love for him would never die.

And it hadn't. But it, too, had gotten misplaced somewhere, being pragmatically replaced by feelings of comfortableness and familiarity. But something was stirring in her. It heated her bones and prickled her tender flesh, and felt the same as when she had been there in Glenn State as a student. When opportunity and social blessing granted Palmer and her a license for intimacy, their smallish apartment hardly needed a heating system for the passion they showed each other constantly, in a thousand ways.

It was almost seven o'clock, and Palmer was not home. If they had reservations for eight at the Inn at Greenbriar, he certainly would be arriving soon.

Daisy put on a slinky, but appropriate dress, something she hadn't worn in quite a while, mostly because it looked younger than she felt. Somehow, tonight she felt younger than it looked. Sitting in front of her dresser mirror, she opened the perfume, touched her fingertip to the bottle top, and dabbed the fragrance here and there on her nape, and, after thinking about it momentarily, into her cleavage. Why not?

Then she sat on the sofa in the living room, and waited.

Palmer pulled into his driveway about seven fifteen, plenty of time, he thought, to change clothes and get to the restaurant. It was dark and chilly. As he stopped short of the house, while still under the shade of an evergreen, he peered out from the warmth of the Volvo at his house, reflecting on the day. He hadn't been around for any of it from Daisy's perspective, of course, but he had made several phone calls to verify that things were taking place as he had arranged. Everything had.

So now, the day had nearly come to a close. Had she understood what he was trying to say? Not that anyone wouldn't assume the obvious, but Palmer wanted her to really understand, to read not only his mind, but his heart and soul, and know that he wanted them to recapture their first love.

He got out, pushed the door to, quietly, and made his way to the front porch. There he paused, and through the voile curtains on the slim window by the door, he tried to see if his wife was in the living room. He thought he saw her figure on the sofa. This was the hour he had waited for.

Palmer reached into his coat, and pulled out a small, white envelope. Silently, he slipped it into a crevice in the storm door. Then he positioned his finger over the creamy glow of the doorbell switch, and pushed twice.

Almost before the sound of the bell inside had stopped reverberating, Palmer's feet touched the bottom porch stair. As he was bounding through the grass of the front lawn, the lump of change in his right front pocket and the keys in his left pocket beat on his legs, ringing like sleigh bells. Mr. Wagner cupped his hands over the noisy metal, muffling the sound, and jogged in short strides toward the shade of the sprawling evergreen. Safely behind it, he controlled his already heavy breathing, resulting partly from the sudden exercise and partly from the adrenalin of nervousness. He peeked around the tree trunk, and watched the door.

A crack of light appeared, and Daisy came through it, opening the storm door, briefly looking one direction and then another, then down for a package perhaps left on the porch. Then it was that she saw the envelope. A slight ripple of joy and anticipation passed through every limb, radiating from her heart. She pulled the little white missive from its place, and fumbled with its flap, as her hands trembled.

Palmer watched from the darkness of the evergreen as she opened the envelope, and took out its handmade contents.

She looked at the red crayon writing on the linen texture card, unevenly cut to fit the small, square enclosure. It bore a simple message of three words, in childlike scrawl:

"I LOVE YOU"

She looked out into the surrounding darkness, toward the deep shadows beneath the evergreen, and knowing who stood there, she formed without voice the words, "I love you, too." And then aloud, Daisy— born Emily Carter—called out softly, "And I always have."

# The Confession

The first clue I had that anything was not right, not normal, not as it always had been, was the cat.

Cruiser was my cat up until two years ago. He got his name because he was a starkly black and white kitten, hence a "black and white," hence a police cruiser, hence—well, you get it by now. Cruiser had been sweet company for eight years until he was felled by some internal abnormality that the vet didn't exactly call cancer but that killed him just the same. His dying with relative suddenness lowered me into a period of grief. I had treasured Cruiser's affection and loyalty. We were buddies. In some ways, he was my best friend.

I know, pathetic. Anyway, as I say, the first clue I had that anything was not as it had been a while ago was Cruiser. I buried him myself at the back of our yard. He shouldn't have been there when I got home, but he was. I shivered.

I should start with what happened earlier in the day. I was driving west on the Memorial highway, that runs through our bedroom community of Grant, heading toward Philipsburg to my law office. The daily trip was something of a contest between me and the traffic signals, which seem to be engaged in a conspiracy to see how often they can stop me at every one of them, lengthening what should be a ten minute trip into twenty-five. The length of the lights is also crazy, from both directions. Traffic on major intersecting roads has to wait more than a minute and a half to cross, and when drivers get their chance, they stream through it urgently, knowing that their opportunity won't last long. It has the effect of making all drivers impatient, leading to rabbit starts and then red light runners.

One particular intersection, an accident waiting to happen, is at Stillworth Road, sort of a loop around Grant. Southbound traffic on Stillworth comes down a modest hill into Memorial highway and appears out of nowhere, the corners of the intersection on that side having stands of trees and undergrowth. People approaching the highway on Stillworth can see the light for about a hundred yards and they know that when the gap between them and traffic in front of them is fifty feet or more, the light will turn yellow, but frequently they count on their speed to get them through the intersection on the tail end of the yellow so they won't have to wait an eternity for the next chance to cross.

Sitting at the red light at Stillworth, I was at the front of the line, followed by a pickup that had come up on me in the last quarter mile and had refused to just pass me. Probably on his cell phone. I glanced up left to the light to see that it had just turned red for Stillworth. A two second delay and my light turned green. One more hurdle passed between me and Phillpsburg. I was hoping I could break the cycle of red lights and get through the other nineteen signals without having to stop again. My theory is that even though engineers probably deny it, there is a coordination of the lights such that either you make them all or you stop at them all.

I gunned it and my little SUV took off through the intersection. I blinked.

I started thinking about times gone by, when I first began driving this stretch and there were precious few businesses or much of anything between Grant and Philipsburg. The garden center, a little church, an old nightclub, a few old houses—they seemed indistinct and hazy, as if viewed through a silk screen, as I passed them now, musing on my early life.

Back in my elementary school years, the highway was a dangerous demarcation between the civilization of our neighborhood and the perils of everything beyond. Later on I sat in the back seat of our car when my mother went shopping in Philipsburg or Daddy took me along to make sales calls and made me stay in the car. I never really experienced the city of Philipsburg before I was a teenager; I was always a little rider who had no one to babysit him at home and so my parents dutifully took me along. But I was never exactly included in the business of the trip. It was never about me.

Later on, when the magical time of teen years arrived, I got my driver's license and finally persuaded the folks to trust me with the beat up second car to take out girls—with an eleven o'clock curfew, of course. I remembered date nights when I took Cathy Williams to the seafood restaurant in Philipsburg and then to the little parking place overlooking the municipal airport. That thought led me to thinking about all the other girls I had dated in high school, lo these seventeen years ago, beautiful, wispy girls with fair skin all of them, blonde or redhead, sparkling eyes and graceful movement. The dream of them was intoxicating. They had come through my life one after the other and left amidst our mutual, waning interest.

Then came college, and Claire. She was not fair of skin, but dark, perhaps Mediterranean in complexion, with curly, long hair that she alternately tied behind her head or put in french braids, which drove me insane. Claire's lips were pouty and sultry and heaven to kiss. And Claire was not wispy. I had always thought that fair, wispy, blonde and auburn lasses were my favorite, but Claire was both full figured and femininely muscular and she touched off something in me that made my legs shiver and my heart race.

Claire seemed indifferent toward me when we first met, my freshman year at State, but when I finally tired of trying to get her attention and forced myself to ask other girls out, she stepped in front of me in my walk to class one day and said, "So, that's it, then? That's all you've got?" It was like something out of that Star Trek where Uhura pretended to be interested in one of the Enterprise's captors, but she played hard to get. The captor finally gave up and she pouted and said, "You don't know how to play the game. I refuse, you come back. You didn't come back." Claire was Uhura. That day, I learned to come back.

I kept coming back, again and again, and my reward—slave as I was to her after six months of the dating pursuit—was finally to become her only thought. When she decided I was the one, it was a life changing event. The girl who had been every State man's dream was suddenly and inexplicably mine. Until the summer between our sophomore and junior years. Claire was killed by a drunk driver in July. We lived two hundred miles apart but were planning to see each other in her hometown the next weekend. Her parents gave me the news over the phone through uncontrollable sobbing.

I almost didn't go back to State the next month. But my father wouldn't let me drown myself in sorrow. Not without compassion for what should never happen to a person, let alone before he is twenty-one, Daddy still insisted that life must go on, that if I laid out now, I might not get to go back when I wanted to, and that all things work together for the good of those who love God and have a purpose in his will. Daddy was a devout, Bible-believing man.

And he was right. I managed to drag myself back to college and to force myself to get up every morning, attend classes and study enough to get passing grades that fall. With the self discipline I developed through the ordeal, the spring semester saw improvement. Senior year was not without its days of painful remembrance, but I finished with honors and went on to law school the next year. When my J.D. was on the wall and I hung my shingle back in Philipsburg, life out in front of me looked at least mildly promising. I hadn't yet recovered my youthful confidence in a bright, wonderful future.

Only one thing hadn't fallen into place for a normal life yet. I hadn't gotten married. In fact, I hadn't even dated after Claire. No doubt, I was terribly out of practice, but once I had my first client, tried his case in the magistrate court and with a flair characteristic of me throughout my life, lost it, I was ready to go out and find a wife.

Instead, she found me. Carly applied for a job as my receptionist slash paralegal, and her being the only one to apply within two weeks of my cheapskate special newspaper ad, but her being quite qualified as well, I hired her. The first week of her job, the two of us sizzled with instant and mounting mutual attraction. On Friday at five, she was packing up and re-packing up and then re-arranging-packing up her things to go, obviously stalling, as I came out into the little reception area on some excuse, really just to look into her bottomless, chocolate eyes and bid her a good weekend. I was wishing it were going to be with me, somehow.

Finally she just blurted out, "Look, let's just drop the pretenses. You and I have been dancing around something all week. You have the hots for me and I got 'em bad for you, and I can't work here and be that way unless we just get it all out in the open and do something about it. I'm going to have to quit if we don't start something together. And if there's some law or some ethical principle that says we can't work together and go out or be together as lovers—" (she said the word and I just about collapsed with need) "—then tell me now. Because the minute you fire me or I quit, you know we're going to wind up in each other's arms."

How long had she worked on that speech? Ironically, it was a lot like what I had been working on for two days.

I muttered in a stunned monotone, "Husbands and wives do the whole lawyer-paralegal thing all the time," wondering if it were actually true. The only case I knew of was the municipal judge in Philipsburg, whose wife was his executive assistant, and nobody said there was anything wrong with it. We stared at each other for about three seconds and then she dropped her bag in the floor and threw her arms toward me. I had already taken the one step between us and we became a single element in a tight embrace and a fiery kiss that engulfed our minds and hearts.

Carly and I became a rumor for about a week, an item for about two weeks, and full bore lovers after a weekend retreat to the mountains nearby where we consummated our secretly conducted vows before a notary in a little wedding chapel alongside the winding two lane road leading up to Perry's Peak. When we came back, I hung a closed sign on the office door for three days while we stayed indoors at my little bungalow, made each other omelets for breakfast, collaborated on sandwiches for lunch-dinner, and watched movies, or left them running in the background as we heated up the sheets in my—our—bed. I drank her in. She consumed me. I burned her up. She exhausted me. We were entwined, mingled, melded, dissolved in one another, wedded as we were in every way. The final piece of my life was in place.

We got a little larger house, bought season tickets at the community theater, set out to eat in every decent restaurant in Philipsburg, adopted Cruiser from the local rescue center, and took annual vacations to interesting places.

It lasted nine years.

I don't really know what happened on my end during that time. I guess the ardor cooled a bit. We still made love, and it was still good, but we had never moved from being lovers to really being friends. It occurred to me more than once ever since she walked into my office that first day that Carly was not far from being Claire, either in the sound of her name or in her looks or her personality. Carly had hair to match her eyes, a rich dark brown, in curls and ringlets that were goddess-like. She was like Waterhouse's Circe, handing the poisoned cup to Ulysses, hair a controlled tangle of mesmerizing darkness, eyes a deep pool with sunlight glints, lips naturally black cherry, and skin the color of fine moccasins. She was athletic without being angular, curvy but not plump. Carly and Claire didn't look anything alike in the face, not so that anyone would confuse one for the other, had Claire been alive to be stood beside Carly in a lineup. But there was no doubt in my mind that Carly touched off something inside me because she was so like Claire in every major way, down to the way she took the initiative to make us a couple where I was reticent and somewhat un-self-assured. And that thought made me realize that if I didn't transition to some deeper oneness with Carly, we might not last.

The transition didn't take place as I had hoped, and

mostly because of me. I didn't find new ways to treasure Carly. I expressed less and less interest in her life other than the moments of it that were spent during our evenings together. After she had worked as my assistant for about a year, I took on a partner, making an additional assistant desirable and interrupting the kind of intimate concourse Carly and I had enjoyed when we were the only two in the office. Carly decided to take a position with Lovette, Burgess & Cole, a large firm across town, one that could pay her much more than I could, and we agreed that all things considered the move was a good idea. We began enjoying the routine that most married couples do, retreating to home at the end of the workday and replaying the events of our continuing lives.

None of that was counterproductive to our marriage. What troubled our union was my melancholy. Daddy died just before mine and Carly's fifth anniversary, and Mother passed on within six months, purely from grief, I think. I didn't realize it at the time, but their deaths unleashed a flood of past griefs that welled up over the next year and submerged me in depression. My past began to surge to the surface: the childhood friend who got run over by a car right beside our house; the favorite uncle who was killed in the crash of his own Piper Cub on a trip down to see us; the fire that destroyed my grandparents' home in Georgia when I was eight, ending all further trips to see them since they moved into a small apartment; Daddy's summary firing from his distribution job and his inability to find equivalent work and pay thereafter. Everything that had a negative impact on my life suddenly seemed to loom large as collective causes of mediocrity and even failure.

When I went to law school, I had envisioned joining a

major firm and making megabucks soon thereafter. Opening my own law office was fulfilling in a way, but I wasn't moving toward that goal of impressive success. I was handling mostly magistrate court cases that paid little if I was paid at all. The few circuit court cases I took on were strung out over a longer period of time and though they generally paid more in lump, proportionate to the weeks or months I spent on them they were not much more remunerative than small claims cases.

In other words, half a decade into my career, it was stalled and held no promise of advancement. I retreated to the past, found much of it marred and disappointing, and I descended into a spiral of negativity, disillusionment and sadness, trying to figure out where I had gone wrong, wondering if there were a way to undo it. In the spring of my life I had investigated the excitement of the young women I courted, dreaming of the time to come when success and love and sex and adventure would fill my days. Then there was Claire, who no sooner had begun to flesh out the dream for me than she died. And while I believed that I had succeeded in doing what my daddy counseled, picking up the pieces and going on with life, in reality I had been treading water, in what turned out to be baseless hope that everything would work out and do so wonderfully. That was what Daddy believed, and what I believed, too, for a long time anyway.

Now, however, I had all but decided it was a lie. I was going to struggle financially, survive barely, disappear into the dim and bland background tapestry of life around me, and die like a candle flame drawing up the last drop of wax. I was going to go out unceremoniously, unsung, unnoticed, never having made a really beneficial difference in the world around me, and never having done anything that I would be proud to look back on and smile at as I went.

Carly realized something was going on as soon as it started. At first, she tried the avenue of positive reinforcement, and when that didn't work, she tried sympathy and encouragement. When I kept becoming more melancholy, she showed indifference. In retrospect, I realize it was feigned—another tactic. She may have believed that I was feeding off the attention my growing depression got me, and that her personal therapy was lengthening the disease. I'm sure now that when she began ignoring my self-disparaging, self-deprecating remarks, her plan was to starve me of the sympathy I was lolling in, as if any sort of attention others paid me was equivalent to their love. Unfortunately for her, I took her indifference as cooling affection, and it made me suspicious.

Had Carly gone to work for Lovette, Burgess and Cole because she had already met someone over there and gotten inappropriately involved? Was it Lovette? He was rumored to be a player. Recently divorced. Increasingly wealthy. Handsome as they come. I had always found Robert Lovette to be boring, though. I didn't know any of the city's lawyers really well, of course—there is more competition than camaraderie between us. Maybe he was much more interesting out of court.

I looked for clues that Carly had gotten involved with someone else. There were no weeks or weekends away that might be subject to suspicion, but after all, Carly and I had gotten involved with each other right there in the office. It could happen over at Lovette's suite of offices, too. There were TV programs about that sort of thing.

And of course, Carly was being indifferent, and then downright impatient with my stagnating condition, my growing tendency to feel sorry for myself—and she was right, because I was. For her own mental health, Carly took up with some neighborhood girls (women, of course, but women my age or younger would always be girls), went here and there with them on Saturdays, and left me to mope or stew, whichever I chose.

Then Cruiser got sick, went rapidly down, and died in my arms at the vet's office. Carly had loved him, too, but I took it with an abnormal kind of grief. His death seemed to symbolize my diminishing hope for joy in life.

Then two lean years came. The glut of attorneys in Philipsburg pitted us all against one another, and my being someone who had never shamelessly promoted myself, my clients were thinning out. Due to the steady success of Lovette, Burgess and Cole, Carly's job was not threatened, although they did dismiss one executive assistant and Carly accepted an increased workload along with some extra hours, for a little extra pay.

Determined to cover all our bills with my income alone, I finally ran out of money before month and went into default on a few credit cards. After a year of trying to rob Peter to pay Paul, it was to the point that we were getting bill collection calls at night, which I managed to answer and claim were wrong numbers. Well, we had in fact gotten bill collection calls for some guy named Alex Hamilton and had threatened to change our phone number. Anyway, finally the calls stopped, but only because, ironically, I was being sued for the amounts due. The one card that got me in trouble was for about ten thousand dollars that mounted up not from luxuries but just for everyday expenses. I hadn't told Carly about it. It was she who was at home one day when a process server came by with a Summons and Complaint and served me via her—which our state allows. When I came home twenty minutes later, I knew something was amiss. It hung in the air like flea fogger.

I try not to remember exactly what went on those next few hours, but the upshot of it is that everything hit the fan. I was exposed, I went on the defensive, and soon I went on the offensive, irrationally trying to blame my actions on Carly. My suspicions of her having some sort of fling came out in a mean, really incomprehensible stream of accusations that stunned her. I took her reaction for the shock of discovery, when in fact she was wounded to the core that I would doubt her love. But she didn't say that at the time. She became silent, retreating into herself, going into a dark place where I could never track her, and where I was not a welcome person. I had no clue what she was thinking. She disappeared into the bedroom, reappeared in a few minutes with a bag, paused at the front door only long enough to say that she would call me after a few days, and then she was gone.

In the days that followed, while deep inside me I knew I should break down, repent of my sins and beg her forgiveness, I didn't. True to her word, she called after three days, and I was home, but I didn't pick up. When the phone rang, I realized I didn't know what to say. Like a good lawyer who doesn't ask a question he doesn't already know the answer to, I didn't want to start a conversation I didn't know how to predict and plan for in advance. I froze when the phone rang, and finally the machine picked up. Carly left me a message telling me when she would call again, and when she did again, two days later, I was accidentally on purpose out for the evening. That time she left no message, just a ten second silence during which I thought I heard a slight sniffle. An evening later, the same thing happened. Two days later, ditto. I regretted deeply not picking up that time and told myself that when she called again in another day or two, I would pick up and blubber and pray for her return.

But Carly didn't call again. I finally realized that she had given me two strikes, and I was now out. I guess I assumed that she would give me another at bat, but she didn't.

Two weeks dragged into a month. Then on a Monday I came home from work to find that most everything that was personally Carly's was now gone. Not furniture, which was odd, because some of it was uniquely hers; but all of her clothes, books, and everyday items, and a few pots and pans, were replaced with empty spaces. Selected sentimental things that had value for us both had been left in place, painful reminders, icons of what had been.

It had been two months now, and by stealthy sleuthing I had found out that Carly was renting a suite in central Philipsburg, not far from her work. I didn't know which suite. I had her cell number, of course, and any time I wanted to call her and try to undo this tragedy that was becoming more permanent every day, I could, but something—pride, no doubt—made me put it off just one more day, just one more day.

And so, I had headed to the office today, fighting with the traffic lights, thinking a thousand thoughts as I drove by the same things as I did every morning and in reverse every evening.

I blinked.

Suddenly I was home.

Oddly enough, this rambling rumination on my life history had taken place with such concentration, such emotional turmoil, such sadness alternating with exhilaration, such a frenzy of potent feelings and powerful images occupying my mind that I didn't remember anything I had done that day since heading down the highway. It wasn't until I opened the door to our—my—house and saw Cruiser that the reminiscing stopped and I really paid attention to my surroundings.

Cruiser looked at me almost wistfully, as if he knew exactly what was going on. Then he turned and disappeared into another room. I stood in the doorway and held my breath. This was not right.

A sudden sensation of intense pressure and pain gripped my entire torso. Heart attack? But it disappeared as rapidly as it had come on.

Then my ears were assaulted with one great wave of white noise and crashing throbs that ended and left a deafening, unimaginable silence.

My eyesight faded and then returned, but an aura appeared around every object and nothing seemed exactly in focus.

Everything went dark again and when light returned, I was not at the house at all. I was unaware of having moved, but now I was at the office, but the furniture was wrong. It was before I had a partner, before Carly took another job.

Then there was a blur, like one of those depictions of a wormhole, rushing away from all around my head—the mountain chapel, the old house, the new house, the car, the cat, faces from restaurants, the hundreds and thousands of witnesses and clients and judges and juries, the neighbors up and down the street who we really didn't know, rain and sunshine, cars rushing by, phones ringing, flashes of light, sirens, chainsaws, red and blue, pulsing yellow, and ripping noises, banging noises, crushing noises, sickening crunching sounds, and then the images all disappeared into a distant point and it stopped.

All was calm.

Then I saw Carly's face. She was standing in front of me, and it seemed as if I had not known her very long, and her lips were moving but I couldn't make anything out until the volume came up and she was saying, "You know we're going to wind up in each other's arms." And then she was gone and her face was replaced with every girl's face I had ever loved and lost or left behind, and all of them morphed into one another, back and forth, until I realized that Carly was the image of them all, their quotient, their sum, and far beyond their equal. That face. That face behind which was the soul that had confronted me with my destiny and grasped me with a possession that was the match for my need, that face to which I had hurled my anger at myself and disappointment in myself in a fit of transference and projection. That face.

That face faded to white and my ears rang from right to left and then together and then stopped, in a beep, a beep, and a long whistle that faded quickly to nothing, and the white went black.

I'm sorry, Carly. I was deeply wrong. I blamed you for my self destruction. You had nothing to do with it. You were my salvation, and I pushed you away. I'm sorry. So sorry—I had only this one thought, and I felt more than spoke it to myself, as I drifted out into a void I did not see, and a deepness I could not fathom.

"I'm sorry." I heard the words this time , but someone else had spoken them, and I felt a tear run into the edge of my lips. It was not mine. It belonged to that face, the face so close now to mine, breathing her sweet breath onto my lips and anointing my lips and cheeks with her kisses, as she spoke back to me.

"I know, I know. Don't worry. I forgive everything." A slight sniffle. "I'll be home when you come back."

Then I slept, dreamlessly and deeply, with the sense that I was smiling, awaiting the promises of dawn.